ANNE COTTRINGER

Singing it

ANDERSEN PRESS · LONDON

First published in 2007 by Andersen Press Limited,
20 Vauxhall Bridge Road, London SW1V 2SA   www.andersenpress.co.uk

British Library Cataloguing in Publication Data available
ISBN 978 1 84270 678 7

Mixed Sources
Product group from well-managed
forests and other controlled sources
www.fsc.org Cert no. TT-COC-2227
© 1996 Forest Stewardship Council

FSC

Typeset by FiSH Books, Enfield, Middx.
Printed in the UK by CPI Bookmarque, Croydon, CR0 4TD

To Alison, Judy, Lynda, Marion and the rest of the group for all your words of wisdom and to all those Wednesday nights at the pub.

Acknowledgements

I am indebted to various websites for their information about Siberian, or as they are more properly known, 'Amur' tigers. I regularly visited the Amur website (http://www.amur.org.uk/tigers.shtml) where, to my horror, I discovered there are only 350 Amur tigers and 35 Amur leopards left in the wild. I make references to this website in the story of *Singing It* but then fictionalised the content of my Amur website for my own purposes. I also spent time on the Wildlife Conservation Society website, where I discovered the story of the legendary Olga (http://www.wcs.org/international/Asia/russia/siberiantigerproject/storyofolga), an Amur Tiger who became the inspiration for my own fictional tigers in the story. Sadly Olga was killed by poachers in 2005.

One

Another new school. As we walked down a long empty corridor, my shoes squeaked on the slippery, shiny floor. The deputy head's heels tapped out quick, staccato clicks as she hurried along in front of me. Occasionally she turned to me with a big smile plastered across her face.

'I'm sure you'll like it here, Flower,' she said hoping that would somehow make me walk faster. She was in a hurry and I was just one more thing she had to sort out.

I tried to make my arms longer inside the sleeves of my new school blazer. My mum had bought it big so 'I could grow into it' and only my fingertips showed below the sleeves. I think she was trying to fool me into believing that we would be in this place long enough for me to grow into anything. She knew that I really wished we could stay in one place for a while.

We usually stayed somewhere for about six months. Then we moved. Ever since something went wrong with the flower shop my parents used to have, we've moved around a lot. My mum and dad sort of collect stuff and sell it in car-boot sales or they get a market stall for a while. We have a van and they haul all their junk around in the back, and when they decide it's time to move on, we stuff everything we own into the back and drive to the next place.

I hate moving all the time. I just make a friend and off we go again. Or sometimes I don't even get a chance to make a friend before I have to pack my stuff into the back of the van and go.

'Almost there.' The deputy head smiled even harder.

I concentrated on trying to keep my cheeks pale. It never worked though. As soon as the deputy head said, 'Class, I'd like you to welcome our new student. This is Flower Power,' heat would swarm up from beneath my shirt and drench my face with sweat.

Flower Power. What do those two words make you think of? Hippies? The Sixties? Well for me, in the twenty-first century those two words are the bane of my life. Fourteen years ago, as my parents cooed and smiled over their brand new baby girl, my father happened to say, 'She's our beautiful little flower.' To which my mother replied (she must have been ga-ga the way women are just after birth), 'Let's call her Flower.'

I'd like to give them the benefit of the doubt and think that they were both so loopy at the moment that they forgot their surname was Power. But I have a terrible suspicion that they thought it was cute to have a daughter called Flower Power.

It's not even like they were hippies (too young) or New Agers (too conservative). I think I was an advertising gimmick. When I was born, they had just opened their florist and were looking for a name for the shop. They named me Flower and they called the shop Flower Power. I'm still confused whether they named me after the shop or the other way around.

Anyway, I want to change my name. Officially. I've tried to do it unofficially. Whenever I go to a new school, I tell them my name is Natalie. Natalie Power. That sounds good. But the records always always let me down. They say 'Flower' and that gets read out no matter how many times I say my name is Natalie. For instance, I told this deputy head that I'm actually called Natalie. She looked a bit distracted when I said it, so I'm not holding out too much hope.

The deputy head turned to me as we reached a door with a small window about shoulder height.

'Ready?'

This time she seemed almost human. As if she might have gone through this herself at one time. I nodded. I didn't trust myself to try and say any words. They would come out all scuffed and scraped. You would think this would get easier, but for some reason it never did.

She pushed open the door and there they were, the thirty faces, just like the last time I did this, six months ago.

I was introduced to the teacher, Miss O'Neill. She smiled. She looked OK. Young, with a short spiky haircut and a little jewelled stud in the side of her nose. For a moment I was mesmerised by her pierced nose and forgot about all those faces, but then I heard those fateful words: 'Class, I'd like you to welcome our new student. This is—'

She checked the piece of paper with my name on it.

'—Flower Power.'

'Peace!' shouted a boy with a huge zit on his chin. He put his fingers up in a peace sign. The class giggled. Why can't anybody come up with anything original? I still couldn't manage to speak so I forced the corners of my mouth up in my facsimile smile.

'Flower, you can have that empty desk at the back there,' said Miss O'Neill.

As I made my way to the back of the class a girl sniggered, 'More like "Weed Power" if you ask me.'

Funnily enough, I'd heard that one before. I think it's on account of my being skinny, with stringy brown hair and – under most circumstances – pale skin. Kind of weedy-looking, really.

'Now Cat,' said Miss O'Neill to the girl sitting beside me. 'I'd like you to be Flower's buddy until she gets used to the school. Show her where everything is and what the school protocol is.'

'Cat's a "Flower Buddy"!' shouted a boy. He had a thick smattering of freckles.

'Shut up, Liam!' snarled Cat.

I shrugged my shoulders and smiled at her. She frowned and turned towards the front of the class. Out of the corner of my eye, I took in the shiny, black hair pulled into a dishevelled pile on top of her head. Her eyes were as black as her hair. She wasn't pretty, but there was something about her. Usually the girls who were assigned to 'look after' me were the ones who didn't have any friends and teachers saw me as a opportunity for them to finally have a friend. I often ended up not having a friend though, because a lot of them were real losers, so I spent a lot of time on my own. Cat didn't look like a loser, but she looked like she sure didn't want me for a friend, so I prepared myself for the life of a loner again.

Two

Cat more or less had her claws out all day. 'Follow me' was pretty well all she said as she stomped from class to class along crowded corridors lined with pastel-coloured lockers. Occasionally the boy who had called her a 'Flower Buddy' would sidle up beside her and flick her bare arm with his fingers or pull a strand of her hair out of the pile on top of her head. His name was Liam. As well as a lot of freckles, he had shaggy red hair. He was not very cool looking.

I kept quiet and vaguely followed Cat.

I was pretty relieved to get home, until I discovered that my parents were already there. I walked into the kitchen and there they were, talking intently to one another across the table. They broke off for a moment to say, 'Oh, hi, Flower. Home already?'

'Yeah.'

And that was it. End of conversation. *Our* conversation. *Their* conversation continued.

Ever since I can remember, my parents have really been totally wrapped up in each other. And as I'm the only other person in this family, I've always felt a bit like an outsider. I've asked for dog or a cat, but my dad is 'allergic' to animals. (I think this is a convenient exaggeration. He just doesn't like them.) What this all means is that I really notice that my parents don't seem to notice me very much, but they don't notice that they don't notice me.

Sometimes I try a mild form of sarcastic humour to point this out them: 'Hi, Mum! Hi, Dad! It's me! Your daughter, "Flower". Remember me? You gave me this really, really dumb name.'

'Flower is a lovely name,' and my mother smiles her benign smile at me, then turns to my father.

'Isn't it, Geoff?'

'Lovely,' he says. 'And we knew that from the moment we saw you.'

And my dad puts his arm around my mum and gives her a squeeze.

Yuk!!

However, I'm not one to wallow in my misfortune. I have other ambitions than to be noticed by my parents. And I had new room to sort out.

Not that I had much sorting out to do. Once I'd rolled out of my bed and put my sheet and duvet on it, there was only my clothes to put away and my pictures to put up (various tigers and my favourite singers). Then I set out my CD Walkman and my CDs which I get second-hand at the car-boot sales. I'm saving up for an MP3 player.

There was also 'my collection'. I hope this flat never gets raided because my collection could put me in jail. You see, I have a collection of library books from every library in every town we've ever lived in. At first I never meant to keep them. I would be in the middle of a really good book when my parents would announce that we were moving again. I couldn't bear to not know what happened in the end so I used to 'forget' to return the book. Once we were a hundred miles away in the next town, the possibility of returning it was pretty remote. Then I started to like the idea of remembering each place we lived in through library books. Now I have a pretty big collection.

My voice sounds really good in this room. It's my new bedroom and it's empty and echoey so my voice comes back to me all big and powerful. The walls are yellow, which I like a lot. My last bedroom had these sort of turdy brown walls which were horrible, but we only stayed in that flat for about six months so I didn't have to put up with it for too long.

You see, my biggest ambition is to be a great singer. I love singing – and it's something that you can do all by yourself. You don't need anyone or anything else. If you play the piano or the guitar, you have to lug it around with you. But your voice is part of you. It's like your mind and your body all mixed into this sound that goes out into the world. Not that my voice goes very far out into the world. Usually it doesn't go beyond the walls of my bedroom and even then my mum and dad ask me to 'keep it down a bit'.

My other great desire is to save tigers from extinction and to that end I have a 'Save the Tiger' website which I run from libraries and various cybercaffs as I don't have my own computer. I have run in four 10K marathons to raise money. In the last one I came 886th out of 892 entrants. I *did* raise £65.74, which is a lot of money.

Three

The next day at school was pretty much like the first day.

Cat would say, 'Buzz off, Juvenile!' to Liam, the tiresome freckled boy, but of course he wouldn't buzz off. He would ask her whether she had heard of this song or that group's new album.

'Maybe . . .' or 'What's it to you?' she would say. They kept this up between classes pretty well all day. Sometimes he would slide his eyes my way to see if I was impressed at his having heard a particular band's latest CD, but they were such crap bands I totally ignored him. When we were going to science, last class of the day, he threw a ball of scrunched-up paper at Cat. It missed and hit me.

'What about you, Weed? You like Bella Armstrong?'

Well as it turns out, Bella Armstrong is absolutely my favourite, favourite singer. She has this voice that can pick you up and carry you like a big wave at the seaside, or it can spill like cream down the back of your throat. And that's just for starters. I have every CD she has ever made – and her voice gets better and better. However, I wasn't going to let this pipsqueak, Liam, know that.

'Maybe,' I said.

'She's crap,' said Cat.

'You haven't even heard her,' said Liam.

''Course I have,' said Cat.

Cat couldn't have heard her or she couldn't say she was

8

crap, but at that point, I couldn't care less whether Cat liked her or not. All I wanted to do was get to the end of the day without another teacher arching their eyebrows at me when they found out my name. Sometimes the other girls looked at me like they might come over and say something to me, even try to be friendly maybe, but Cat's snarly face kept them pretty much at bay. Maybe Miss O'Neill thought I might be the one to tame her. Well, she was wrong.

However, at the end of the second day, when I said, ''Bye,' Cat said. 'See ya tomorrow.' I nearly fell over. For her it was positively friendly.

Four

After school, I went to the library which turned out to be quite close to our flat. It was one of those new-fangled ones with lots of glass that pretend they aren't really libraries because they think nobody wants to go to a library these days. It wasn't even called a library. It's called 'The Knowledge Store'.

Anyway, I like these new ones. They've got tons of DVDs, CDs and loads and loads of computers. Unfortunately they tend to have the same old crabby women working in them – like the one today who told me to be quiet when I was at the computer. I wasn't talking, but ever since that boy Liam had mentioned Bella Armstrong, her song 'Soul Searcher' was running through my head. You know the way you can't get a song out your head?

Bella Armstrong has this way of seeming to start way up somewhere in the blue, blue sky and then swooping down. Then her voice sort of digs through the earth into this dark, warm place. She doesn't have one of those horrible breathy female voices that go all quavery and make them sound helpless. Hers is strong even when she's singing about something sad like losing your boyfriend. I don't know what it's like to lose your boyfriend (I've never had one), but I'm sure it feels like you feel when you listen to this song.

Anyway, I love this song and I couldn't help humming it to myself while I was cruising various websites. The librarian (or maybe I should call her the 'storekeeper') didn't seem to appreciate this musical accompaniment and told me I could sing for my supper elsewhere. I thought this was a bit rich given all the pinging and zinging coming from computer games that kids were playing almost next to me. I stopped for a while but the song kept bursting through when I wasn't thinking and every time she gave me the big glare.

My Save the Tiger website has had thirty-eight hits since I last checked a few days ago. I started it three years ago and sometimes I think that maybe I've outgrown it. It's sort of a kid thing, but I just love tigers and through the website I exchange pictures with people all over the world. My favourite tiger is the *panthera tigris altaica*. Otherwise known as the Siberian tiger. There are only 150–450 of them left. They are so huge and powerful. It practically makes me cry when I think of them, all alone, padding through the forests of Russia. And when there is news of one of them being killed, well, I feel s-o-o-o depressed for days. But today I found a great photo in my mailbox of a Siberian from this girl, Erin, who lives in Minnesota in America. It took my mind off the horrors of these first days at school.

I wasn't in any hurry to get back to the flat so I sort of wandered down the High Street. I was humming again, but my mind had somehow switched into another Bella Armstrong song – a real upbeat one about getting ready to go out on a Saturday night. Then without realising it, I must have started singing it, because suddenly an arm was thrust in front of me holding a bunch of flowers.

'Singing like that deserves a bouquet!' said a voice. An

old crackly voice. A bit like old leather. It belonged to a slightly hunched old guy with a big grin and a missing tooth. He had one of those Sherlock Holmes hats that was sitting sideways on his head so the two peaks stuck out on either side of his head rather than front to back.

'Go on! These are for you!' he said. 'I love to hear a voice singing a happy song like that.'

I think I must have just stood there, looking gormless and surprised, because he said, 'What's the matter? Would you rather have some lilies? I don't think they suit the song, but you can have lilies if you'd rather.'

He pointed to a big bucketful of lilies that was part of the display on his flower stall.

'No,' I said. 'These are lovely. But, I'm sorry, I don't have any money.'

'Forget your money,' he said. 'These are a present.'

'Thank you,' I managed to squawk. I breathed in this really heady smell. These were potent.

'What are they?'

'Freesias,' he smiled.

'My parents used to have a flower shop,' I said.

'Then you should know what they are.'

'It was a long time ago.'

'Well, enjoy them. And thanks for the song!'

I felt a bit silly walking down the street carrying a big bunch of flowers. But not nearly half as silly as I did a few minutes later. I was thinking about the old man and not paying much attention to anyone around me when I came upon two people in front of me walking along with their arms around each other, talking together and occasionally kissing. That was yucky enough, but a moment later I realised they were my parents! Sometimes my parents are so over the top. They act like newlyweds, but they aren't. My aunt says they're stuck in their teenage years. She disapproves of them, like I do.

They were walking really slowly. I felt really dumb having to walk along slowly behind them so I decided to pass them. They probably wouldn't notice me anyway. Just as I had pulled in front of them, and surprise, surprise, they hadn't noticed me (I put it down to the unfamiliar uniform), I could feel someone coming along beside me who must have also just passed them. When I glanced towards the person – it was Cat.

'Get a load of those two! Aren't they a bit old for that?' she said in an ultra loud voice so they could hear. And of course they did, and of course they looked in our direction.

'Flower!' cried my mum.

'You know her?' said Cat.

'How was school, darling?'

Five

You can imagine what school was like the next day. Not only was I the new girl with a stupid name, but I had parents who snogged in public. All day long, other students huddled in whispering groups and then stole looks in my direction.

I had to put up with Liam doing loud kissing sounds at me between classes. As for Cat, she kept saying stupid things like, 'Oh Flower, could you go make us a cup of tea while we have a snog.' I refused to talk to her.

Thanks, Cat. Your discretion is gratefully appreciated.

I hated my parents sometimes! Why couldn't they just be normal? It was OK when I could just ignore them and they ignored me, but then they did stuff like this. And they just don't see it. They can't imagine that it might be slightly embarrassing to have your mum and dad acting like teenagers on the street. They couldn't understand why I stomped off home. When I suggested that their rather unseemly behaviour would be the major topic of conversation the next day in school, my mother told me I shouldn't let people's petty minds get under my skin. I should be above all that. Easy for her to say that.

When Miss O'Neill asked me how I was getting on I just said, 'Fine.' What else can you say? That your parents snogged in public and now everyone in the class knows and is making your life a misery. That Cat, who was so supposed to make your life easier, takes great pleasure in seeing you squirm.

'If you have any problems, you can come and see me,' was Miss O'Neill's lame offer. Don't teachers know that you never go to them? What are they going to do? You can just imagine the scene: 'Now, Class. Flower tells me that you aren't being very nice to her. I want us all to put our heads together and think of ways to make her feel more at home in her new school.'

Besides making a normal person puke, this kind of scene would mean you'd get scalped on the way home from school. A teacher did once do something very similar to this to me. Except it was even worse. She announced to the class that it was very difficult being the new girl and that they should help me realise my 'flower power'. Excuse me? I think she thought she was being quite clever with words but the results were pretty disastrous. Thank God we stayed there for an even shorter time than we usually stay somewhere.

At the end of the day Cat ran off with two other girls, Tamsin and Kerry. She blew me a kiss goodbye. Very funny.

If I knew my parents weren't at home, I would've gone back to the flat, but you never knew when they might be there. Sometimes they would get home early and sometimes they might be out till about eight o'clock. I certainly didn't want to see them, so I decided not to risk it. I decided to wander through the town.

I think I've spent a lot of my life doing this. Wandering through strange town centres on my own. You notice more when you're on your own. If you're with someone you get caught up with them and your conversation. But it gives you a chance to do a lot of daydreaming. Like today, I was imagining what it would be like to have Bella Armstrong as a big sister. She's too young to be my mother so she would have to be my sister. I imagined that something happened to my parents and that Bella Armstrong sort of adopted me. I would go on tour with her and keep her entertained on those long flights. I'd help her get ready for concerts. I'd lay out her clothes, and do her hair for her. She has sliced honeydew melon and orange sherbet before every concert. I'd make sure she got good ripe melons and I'd cut them up just the way she likes. She would insist that we share hotel rooms because she felt lonely without me. I was luxuriating in all these thoughts when I realised I was standing in front of a music shop with a display of her CDs in the window. Like I said, I have them all, but I decided to go in and check out the place.

It turned out to be a great shop. It was called the Bass Clef and there were lots of listening posts with a huge choice of stuff to listen to. I got lost in a rap version of a Bob Dylan song (I know about him from my grandparents – they are completely nuts about him). I guess I had my eyes closed because when I opened them up, a couple of listening posts away there were these two boys who hadn't been there before. They each had headphones on and were sort of dancing to the music. They were gorgeous, especially the taller one. He had shiny black hair that curled around his ears, and chocolatey brown eyes with lashes so long that you could see them from where I was standing. And great lips that curled up at the corners so he looked like he was smiling even when he wasn't. The other one was rougher looking, with short spiky hair that he'd hennaed at the tips. They were dressed in the most cool way — baggy jeans, ripped T-shirts and old track shoes. They looked like they were a year or two older than me. Year 10 or maybe Year 11. I couldn't take my eyes off them. I tried to sort of smoulder my eyes in case one of them looked my way, but as soon as one of them did I whirled around and turned my back to them. Then I wondered why I'd bothered. They would never notice a weed like me.

Six

After about a week, Cat was able to drop the pretence that she was my 'buddy'. A week was considered long enough for a new girl to learn the ropes and make new friends. It was a relief not to have Cat's surly presence beside me between classes anymore. And with her went Liam's maniacal comments and attempts to be funny. Although in a funny way, I missed him.

And I have discovered a couple things. Firstly, that the gorgeous boy from the music shop was called Ashok. His friend was Lenny and they had a band that was considered the coolest band in the school. I overheard Cat, Tamsin and Kerry talking about them and gathered from their giggling that Cat fancied Ashok something terrible.

I also discovered this great tree out in the fields that I could see from my bedroom window. It's a huge old oak tree that stands out in the middle of the field all by itself. I love to go and sit underneath it. The weather is still at that leftover-from-summer stage. Warm and balmy. Sometimes I just daydream, but a lot of the time I sing. I could sing as loud as I wanted to most of the time because hardly anyone goes out there, just the occasional dog walker.

And I have a friend. Mick. The old man at the flower stall. Whenever I used to walk by his stall, he used to call out, 'It's the Diva of Don Valley!' (The town is in the Don Valley). And every Tuesday he gives me a bunch of freesias. It turns out he has had his flower stall all his life.

He inherited it from his father. He's a bit sad, because his two kids, and now his grandchildren, live in London and aren't at all interested in the flower stall. When he discovered my name was Flower he was so chuffed.

'Perfect!' he said. 'You and my stall are made for one another.'

I think he sees me as a possible future tender of the flower stall. I explained that I'm going to be a famous singer when I grow up.

'I don't doubt that!' he chuckled. 'But it's always good to have something you can fall back on.'

He used to play saxophone in a dance band that played all the big halls in the local area. Swing, big band music, and jazz. I don't know what he's talking about, but he's promised (or threatened, as the case may be) to give me some of his records for me to take home and listen to. When I explained I don't have a record player, he said he would burn me some CDs. He wants me to hear Billie Holiday and Ella Fitzgerald. Real singers, he says. But it turns out he likes Bella Armstrong and he rates her right up there with them. Now I can't wait to hear Billie and Ella.

'The Knowledge Store' has books as well as computers, and I've read some great books recently. *Wuthering Heights* was the most amazing. There's this great girl in it called Cathy who has this thing for this dark and dangerous Heathcliff, who is a sort of adopted by her father. The first part is all wild and passionate and on the moors. That was the best bit. I told my mother about the book. I don't usually volunteer this kind of info, but she asked me what I was reading and she was impressed that

I'd read it. She said she didn't read it until she was eighteen. I don't really care if she's impressed or not, especially after she made me come with her and my dad to a Saturday market and I had to look after our stall while they went wandering around the market arm in arm. When I complained my mum said they had to check out what the competition was like. She tried to buy me off with a *No Redemption* CD but it didn't work. They're a crap band.

Seven

Something very weird happened the other day. I was in 'The Knowledge Store' doing some work on my Save the Tiger website when I became aware of this familiar smell. Not smell in the nasty sense, but in the scent sense. It seemed to be floating in the air just over my right shoulder and when I looked round, there was Cat looking over my shoulder at the screen.

'Do you mind?' I asked.

'What a great picture of a *panthera tigris tigris*,' she said.

'A what?'

'Bengal Tiger.'

'I know it's a Bengal Tiger. I'm just surprised that you know the Latin name.'

'Is that the Save the Tiger/Panthera Five website?'

'Yes. I've just got a few more pics in so I'm posting them up.'

'What!? That's your website?'

'Yeah.'

'I can't believe it! I've been going there since it started. It's my favourite cat website of all time! You get such cool pictures!'

'I've got contacts all over the world now. We share them and whenever I get a really good one, I post it up.'

'And I know what your favourite tiger is,' she said. Her black eyes were all shiny and smiling. This was a Cat I hadn't seen before, but her name was starting to make a lot of sense.

'*Panthera tigris altaica*,' I said before she could.

'It's mine too!' cried Cat. 'Did you see that TV programme a few weeks ago about them? Those horrible fat poacher guys. It made me want to go out there and be a volunteer ranger.'

I couldn't believe it. Cat loves Siberian tigers too.

'And it was so great when they caught that guy who was trying to export that tiger pelt!'

'Yeah. And don't you just hate how they're breeding white tigers to make them into tourist attractions?'

'With all those genetic problems? It's cruel. I nearly went on a demo at that zoo which is doing it, to protest, but in the end my mum wouldn't let me go.'

Cat sat down in the seat next to me.

'Have you seen the DVD they have here? It's a special about Bengals?'

'No.'

'C'mon. We can get it out and watch it together. Do you have a DVD player at your house?'

'Yeah.'

'Great! Can I come over tonight and watch it with you?'

I wasn't so sure I wanted Cat in the house after the last encounter with my parents. I didn't trust them to behave.

'Why don't we go to your house?' I said. 'My parents might be making wild passionate love on the sofa. It could prove a bit embarrassing.'

Cat laughed. That was a relief.

'My parents always watch *Accident and Emergency* on Wednesday nights. There's no way they would let us near the TV. And it's really noisy with all my brothers and sisters.'

'Well . . . my place is a bit tricky, but maybe this could be one of my parents' late-getting-home nights.'

'It's free to take out for a night,' Cat said hopefully.

'I guess, if we go now . . .'

'Great!' said Cat. 'I'll sign out the DVD on my card.'

On the way back to the flat, we talked about tigers, naturally. Cat turned out to be pretty knowledgeable. And she turned out be a completely different person than she was at school. Not at all sulky and sarcastic.

'I've never met anybody else who likes tigers as much as I do,' said Cat. 'And I still can't believe that the website is yours. It's just too cool.'

She took out her mobile.

'Look! I've got some really good tiger pics on my phone. I downloaded them straight onto it.'

She had a few I'd never seen including a really cute one of a huge Bengal cub.

'Any on your phone?' she asked.

'I don't have a phone,' I said. 'I lost my old one and I haven't got a new one yet.'

And unlikely to get one either, because I'd never had a phone. I felt bad lying to Cat, but I think I was the only kid in the school who didn't have a mobile. My parents said I didn't need one. They argued that it only made you a target for muggers.

'What? No phone? What if I want to phone you?'

'Landline?'

'Boring,' said Cat.

My parents were out. Fingers crossed they wouldn't come back for a while. We sat together on the worn-out old sofa in the living room where my parents usually sat. It felt kind of funny, sitting with Cat on *their* sofa – like I was trespassing on my parents' territory. It smelled a bit like my mum's perfume. She used to lie here watching television with her feet on my dad's lap. I never sat on it with them. There was an old armchair where I sat. But now I was sitting where my mum normally sat, and Cat was at my dad's end of the sofa.

The only other furniture in the room was the TV, VHS player and DVD player. I had never really noticed how empty it was. Somehow having this other person witness your space was a bit like revealing something that's private. Like taking your clothes off in public. Not that I ever did that, I only had dreams about it.

'Not much furniture,' said Cat.

'So?'

'I like it,' said Cat. 'Our house is so crowded.'

'We'll be getting some more,' I said. 'When we settle in.'

Who was I trying to kid? We never had very much furniture on account of moving so much. This sofa had been tied to the roof of the van more times than I can remember.

'I like it like this,' said Cat.

The DVD was great, just as Cat had said. She was really pleased to show me something that I hadn't seen before, because I had pretty well tracked down all the tiger stuff there was.

'That's the fifth time I've seen it,' said Cat.

'It's good. More sophisticated than a lot of tiger stuff.

24

A lot of it's geared towards kids.'

'Yeah. People think you're babyish if you like tigers,' said Cat. 'It's a drag.'

'I'm in email contact with tiger conservationists and zoologists. They don't talk down to you like a lot of the websites.'

I was bragging now and I could tell Cat was impressed. Not usually a reaction I can elicit from anyone.

'What's your real name?' I asked.

'Guess.'

'Catherine?'

'Sort of. Katerina. My mother is into exotic versions of names.'

'I like Katerina. Better than Catherine. It's so snobby and stuck up.'

'I hate Katerina!' she said. 'For a while they tried to call me Kitty because I always pretended I was a cat when I was small, but I hated that too. I hate the letter "K" – too many cute names begin with K.'

'My real name is Natalie,' I said.

'Really? Why are you called Flower, then?'

'My stupid parents,' I said. 'I want to be called Natalie though.'

'I'll call you Natalie,' said Cat.

'Maybe you could start a trend,' I said.

I was getting worried that my parents would come back soon and I really didn't want Cat to be there when they did.

'Do you want to out and get some fish and chips? I've got some supper money that my parents left me in case they were late.'

'No thanks. I better get home or my mum will go mad. We eat at seven o'clock and if I'm late she'll kill me.'

Cat gathered up her stuff, and as she went out the door she turned and said, 'Maybe we can get those fish and chips after school tomorrow?'

Eight

'Dandelion Weed!'

Oh, give me a break.

'C'mere, Cat, and let's see if you like dandelion weeds!' chanted Kerry and Tamsin holding a dandelion flower under their chins. They were becoming real pains. It seems they didn't like Cat and me being friends. Cat came and sat next to me in a lot of classes and we walked together between classes and talked – not just about tigers, but about lots of things. Kerry and Tamsin were jealous. They started calling me 'Dandelion Weed' after they saw me give Cat a photograph of a Sumatran tiger. I don't think they knew the difference between a lion and a tiger. I ignored them most of the time. I mean how childish can you get? 'Dandelion Weed.' At least 'Weed' on its own has a bit of street cred. Cat was more bothered because they were already her friends and she didn't really want to lose them.

Finally, though, after a while she said, 'Well, if they want to be like that . . .' She turned her back on them and looped her arm through mine and we walked off.

It felt so good. Cat was choosing me over Kerry and Tamsin who had been her friends since primary school.

'Don't worry, Flower. I've outgrown them,' she declared.

As much she tried, Cat could never remember to call me Natalie. I gave up correcting her.

One night she came back to our flat after school and my parents were there. I was about to turn around and go right back out the door, but decided I had to face this one. I introduced Cat to my parents, who were busy with their heads together sorting out some deal they were doing with chairs from a café that had gone out of business.

'Oh, hello,' said my mum.

My father just smiled this kind of indulgent smile he has whenever I bring anyone around.

'Nice to see Flower with a friend,' he said.

Oh pleeeze!! I hustled Cat out of the room.

'There's some ice cream in the freezer compartment. Your favourite,' called my mum.

I opened the freezer. Butter pecan. My father's favourite, not mine.

'Want some ice cream?'

'No thanks,' said Cat. 'I'm watching my waistline.'

'What?' I snorted. 'What for?'

She kind of, almost, turned the slightest shade of pink. Interesting. Because Cat wasn't the blushing type. She didn't answer.

'We can go to listen to some music in my room,' I said. I was trying to give Cat a bit of a musical education. She had some appalling taste, including a penchant for boy bands which she no doubt shared with the likes of Kerry and Tamsin.

'So who is it?' I asked as I shut my bedroom door.

'What do you mean?'

'Who are you watching your waistline for?'

'No one.'

'Is it Liam?' I teased her.

28

She laughed and curled her lip.

'That little twerp?'

'Go on. There is someone you fancy. I can tell.'

She pulled the clip out of her hair and the black pile tumbled down. When she did that I knew she was going to let me in on her secret.

'You know that guy in Year 11? The one with the band?'

'Which one?' I feigned ignorance.

'The tall, drop-dead gorgeous one with the long eyelashes?'

'I'm not sure,' I lied. 'What's his name?'

'Ashok.'

'I think I know who you mean.'

Of course I knew. He was the one I saw at the record shop. And every time I saw him at school I tried to smoulder my eyes, but he never noticed me.

'Yesterday on the way home from school, he was walking behind me with that friend of his, Lenny. As they went by, he smiled at me. He lives just a couple of streets over from me and sometimes I see him at the corner shop.'

'Guess you'll be hanging out there every night, then.'

'Do you think I should get my belly button pierced?'

'What?!'

'It looks so cool and if I can lose some weight . . .'

'Cat! You don't need to lose any weight!'

'You can say that! Look at you. You're so nice and thin.'

'Skinny, you mean. Believe me, you don't want to be thin and weedy like me.'

Cat has what is called a 'full figure'. She's not fat but she's sure not skinny. I would like to be like her.

'Ashok might notice me with a nice, flat stomach and a pierced bellybutton.'

I was hoping that someday he might notice *me*, but I didn't have a chance next to someone like Cat.

'Maybe.'

'C'mon, Weed. Don't you think he's gorgeous?'

'I guess he's kind of cute.'

For some reason, I didn't want Cat to know that I fancied him like mad. I couldn't tell her about that day at the record shop when I first spotted him.

'We could stalk him,' I suggested.

'Sneak up on him and then pounce!' she giggled. 'What about you? Fancy anyone? Lenny, maybe?'

'Give me a break!' I snorted.

'He's a great drummer.'

'As drummers go.'

'What! You don't like drummers?' she laughed.

'Guitar players are more my style.'

'Then Liam's the man for you.'

'Liam?'

'He plays guitar.'

'For a band?'

'No way. By himself. In case you haven't noticed he's really into music.'

'I had sort of. From the very first day. But he's such a pain. And he fancies you like mad.'

'No way.'

'Why do think he bugs you so much?'

'You're mad.'

Cat went over to the big window and stared down the street to the fields beyond...I put on a Bella Armstrong CD. I was going to put on one of the Billie Holiday CDs that Mick from the flower stall had given to me to listen to, but I thought it might be just a bit of a leap for Cat – from boy bands to Billie Holliday. Mick had been right about her. Billie had this voice like I'd never heard before. Sometimes for some reason it made me think of eating liquorice. And a lot of the songs were so sad and lonely. You just felt it in your guts. I did anyway. And then there was this one – 'Georgia on My Mind' – that her voice made so sweet and homesick all at the same time. She had been born when her mother was thirteen years old! One year younger than me! That would be so weird to have a mother who was only thirteen. And it would be equally weird to have a daughter at thirteen!

Anyway I put Bella Armstrong's first album on instead, because it is a good mixture of upbeat songs and the more bluesy type stuff. I knew Cat had said that Bella Armstrong was crap to Liam that very first day of school, but I don't think Cat had really listened to her.

'I really like your room,' said Cat. 'I have to share mine with my younger sister and it's such a drag. I can't tell you. She's always there. I never have any time on my own.'

'I never have any time *not* on my own,' I said.

'What about your parents?'

'You've seen them,' I said. 'They're just totally, madly in love with one another. You'd think it would wear off after all these years.'

'I think it's kind of nice, really,' said Cat. 'I know I teased you about them, but it's better than my parents. All they do is fight all the time.'

'It gets kind of lonely, sometimes,' I said.

'Hey, this is a good song,' said Cat. The second track was playing.

I smiled.

'It's Bella Armstrong.'

Nine

'Who wants to belong to a stupid choir?' I said, my voice acid with sarcasm.

Cat and I stopped in front of the clubs and societies notice board. Tamsin and Kelly were putting their names down to be in a choir that Miss O'Neill was setting up.

'Chance to be "Nearer my God to Thee!"' sneered Cat.

'You've got it totally wrong!' said a voice behind us. Miss O'Neill stepped up.

'If you actually read the whole thing, you might notice that it isn't a choir. It's a singing club. We'll be doing jazz and rock. Some of the boys are into hip-hop and rap. It's not going to be everyone standing in rows wearing white blouses and black skirts. We'll break down into groups...solos. It's a chance for you to sing. And it's mixed. Girls and boys.'

'I'm not too hot on organised songfests,' said Cat.

'Me neither,' I said. I felt like I should back Cat up on this for some reason. I mean I just love to sing but it didn't really appeal, this idea of singing with other people. And especially not in front of them.

'I'll bet you're both good singers,' said Miss O'Neill.

'Not me,' said Cat. 'My mum says I sound like a dying feline.'

'Sometimes mothers are not the best judge of these things,' said Miss O'Neill. 'How about you, Flower?'

I wasn't sure what to say. I think I'm a good singer, and I want to be a really great singer, but then I've never really sung in front of anyone. My mum has only ever asked me to keep it down. Somehow in my imagination, I'm going to be a really great and famous singer without having to actually sing in front of people. For me, singing is a private, deep down thing.

'I'm not really into organised stuff,' I said.

'It would be a chance for you get to meet some more people,' said Miss O'Neill.

Except that Cat's my friend now. Why would I want to meet any other people?

'I'm OK,' I said.

'Well, if either of you change your minds, we meet on Tuesdays and Thursdays after school,' said Miss O'Neill. She reached and pinned up another A4 sheet with space for more signatures. I noticed in the little gap between her blouse and her skirt that opened up that she had a pierced bellybutton.

I looped my arm through Cat's and we hurried away.

'Did you see her bellybutton?' I said when we were far enough away.

'Yeah! Cool or what! She's such a cool teacher. I like Miss O'Neill. Why couldn't she run a drama group or something like that?'

'I couldn't act,' I said. 'I'd turn red before I even got the words out.'

'I love acting,' said Cat.

I could imagine Cat up there on a stage, all big gestures and a loud strong voice. I wanted to tell Cat that I loved singing, but somehow I was afraid to. I was afraid she might giggle about it and then ask me why I didn't sign up for Miss O'Neill's singing group, when one of the reasons I didn't was that I just wanted to spend time with Cat. That, and my total fear of performing in front of other people.

'Oh, God! Look who's coming down the corridor!' Cat tightened her grip on my arm.

I could have been blind and known who was coming down the corridor. There was only one person who could get Cat so worked up.

'Liam!' I giggled.

'Pretend we're talking about something important and we don't see them,' said Cat.

'Why?'

'You don't want them to think we're interested?'

'But aren't you?'

'Don't be such a dolt, Weed!'

'Anyway, they're interested in you, not me.'

'Say something else!'

Ashok and Lenny were about three metres away.

'You know that discussion we were having about justice and reconciliation in class the other day? Well, I think that in order for justice to be done, people shouldn't be asked to just forgive and for—'

'Hey!' said Ashok.

'Hey!' said Lenny.

'Hi!' said Cat.

By the time I had a chance to mumble out a 'Hi' they had already sauntered past, in their slow, cool way.

'I was just in the middle of a really important thought back there,' I said.

'Oh, Weed! They talked to us!'

'"Hey!" could not be exactly considered talking to us. And in any case, that "Hey" was directed at you.'

'No it wasn't. I'm sure I saw Lenny giving you the eye!'

'Bollocks!'

'Isn't Ashok just so unbelievably dreamy?' asked Cat.

'He's OK,' I admitted. 'But I bet he has a girlfriend.'

'Maybe it's about time he dropped her, then.'

Whether he did or he didn't, neither of us had much chance with him. I couldn't even look at him back there. I would have turned red to the roots of my hair. Even my hair would have turned red. I wish I could be like Cat. I don't think she has ever gone red in her life. And she thought she was in there with a chance.

'Should we go to the library and check your website before we go back to my place?' said Cat.

I loved the way Cat was so interested in my website. She said she could never *not* be interested in tigers. When I asked her what she would do if Ashok didn't like them, she said she would show him my website and then he would change his mind. I loved her for that.

Anyway, I had been asked over to Cat's for supper that night. It wasn't as if Cat was very enthusiastic about the idea, but she had come over to our place so often, she felt she had to reciprocate. She said suppers were a nightmare in her house and you never got enough to eat because of her piggy brothers. I was looking forward to some lively company for a change.

Ten

'Katerina! Stop slouching! Sit up and eat properly!' said Cat's mum through the tumble of curls that kept falling in front of her eyes. I could feel Cat's resentment as she adjusted herself slightly in her chair. She wouldn't look at me.

'Mum! Andreas took some of my chicken!'

'I just took back the piece you took from me!'

'I don't like peas.'

'Why can't we ever have apple juice? Why does it always have to be orange juice?

'Ouch! Mum! Julio pulled my ear!'

'Carl, can't you do something to control your children?'

I'd never been a warzone like this before. Word grenades were lobbed at each other over the serving dishes. Complaints scattered like shrapnel in every direction. The occasional burst of machine-gun laughter aimed to annoy. Still, it was better than the dead zone which is what my evening meals were like.

'I bet things are much quieter at your house.' Cat's mother raised her voice above the din of battle.

'Mum! Can I have that piece of chicken?'

'Ivana's already had an extra piece!' wailed Cat's younger brother. I think his name was Julio. The others were Ivana, Magdalena and Andreas. What a strange collection of names. It seemed like Cat's mother was trying to create a kind of European Community of names. As if that would lead to peace.

'I was trying to talk to Cat's friend,' said Cat's mum. 'Now be quiet for once!'

She looked at me, expecting an answer to her question. I didn't think anyone at this table actually followed a line of conversation so I wasn't really ready with an answer.

'Uh, well. It's pretty quiet at our house. Too quiet, really.'

'Well, can I come and have meals at your house, then?' laughed Cat's mother.

'Mum!' moaned Cat.

'What's the matter with *you*?' Her mum glared at Cat. 'Leave Flower alone.' She turned to me. 'You don't want my mother cross-examining you, do you?'

I hated getting into these no-win situations with these kinds of questions. Someone was going to be miffed no matter what I answered. I felt in this case, I had to be polite to Cat's mother.

'It's OK,' I said.

'It's not!' said Cat. 'You told me before you came that you hoped my mother wouldn't ask a lot of snoopy questions.'

'But I didn't mean—'

'What did you mean then?' said Cat.

Now everyone was looking at me. And the table was silent for the first time. I could have throttled Cat. I could feel the warmth spreading up from under my collar.

'Flower's turning red!' cried Ivana.

'Shut up!' said Cat.

'Don't tell your sister to shut up!' said Cat's mother.

'Let's get out of here!' cried Cat and she grabbed my hand. She stood up and pulled me towards the door.

'Uh! Thanks for dinner! It was really tasty!' I called over my shoulder. Cat stormed towards the front door. She slammed the door behind us.

'I hate my family!'

'Yeah! Well, don't take it out on me!' I said.

'You wanted to stay there and listen to all that crap?'

'It wasn't that. It was you! Like what am I s'posed to say? I mean – telling your mum I didn't want her to snoop?! How could you do that to me?'

I watched Cat's nostrils dilate. She had these perfectly formed little curves that flared like some kind of undersea creature. She bit her lip.

'I'm sorry, Weed. I just get so annoyed with them. I started to lump you together with them.'

'In some ways I'm flattered.'

'You're lucky. You don't have to put up with that every night. Why does my mum insist we all eat together? It's such a nightmare!'

'It's not so bad.'

'Let's go to your place. At least we can get some peace and quiet.' Cat put her arm through mine.

'Uh, well...' I didn't move.

'I told my parents I would be at your place until about half past eight.'

'So?'

'It's only half past seven. So, they're expecting to have the house to themselves.'

'Oh, c'mon. They won't mind. What are they going

to be doing? Having sex hanging from the chandelier?'

I didn't answer.

'Go on! They wouldn't, would they? Besides, you don't even have a chandelier.'

Cat began walking down the road.

'I wish I had some way of warning them we were coming.'

'You're just being paranoid. They're parents for God's sake.'

'Yeah, but my parents are different.'

Eleven

'Wait a minute, Cat!' I said when we got to our front door. 'Let me at least rattle my keys a bit to warn them!'

'I don't believe this!' said Cat, sighing one of her elaborate drama-queen sighs.

I rattled the keys. I rattled the doorknob. I rattled the keys again.

'Weed!' cried Cat. Very impatiently. And with that, she turned the knob, pushed the door open, and stepped past me into front hall.

'Who-o-o-o's that?' asked my mum's startled voice.

Cat called out and strode into the living room, full of Cat enthusiasm. Cat really liked my parents now. I think because they were so completely different from her own. And they always seemed to have more time for her than they had for me. So she usually stopped to talk to them for a bit while I hurried away to my room. Anyway she plunged ahead before I could stop her. Well, I did warn her.

She stopped short.

'Uh, sorry. Really sorry!' she cried.

I could hear a scuffling and some muffled cries or something like that. I didn't listen very hard. I didn't want to hear. I didn't want to know. I didn't want to be there. I had warned Cat. Now in a loud and deliberate voice as if she was speaking to people who didn't speak English very well, she said, 'We are just on our way to Flower's room. Sorry to disturb you.'

Luckily I could cut through the kitchen to get to my room. Cat and I almost ran straight into one another in the short little corridor that led to my room. She made a face and hurried into my room. She threw herself onto my foam mattress. I flopped down beside her. Humiliation or what?! My parents are just too much.

'You were right about your parents!' gasped Cat.

'Don't say a thing! And please! Spare me the details!' I wailed.

'I think they were "doing it"!'

'Cat!'

'Sorry!'

There was a pause.

'I just didn't really believe parents did that sort of thing. I'm sure mine don't.'

'How do you think you got here?' I asked.

'That was a long time ago. I don't think they do it anymore.'

'Look, I don't even want to think about it,' I said.

I closed my eyes. Yellow and red blobs pulsed across my eyelids. They hurt. But I didn't want to open my eyes. I mean, how could I even look at my parents after this? And they would try to be jolly about it. As if it was a joke. I wish they would run away from home. I would, but I didn't want to leave Cat.

There was only one thing left to do. I got my favourite Bella CD and put it on my CD Walkman. I gave Cat one of the earphones and I took the other. It wasn't ideal but it would do. I put on 'Wounded Bird'. Those flighty, soaring high notes and then the plunge down the scale into a minor key and the depths of despair. It felt so good to feel so bad. I played it about ten times. By the fifth time, Cat handed the other earphone over to me and started reading one of my library books.

When I'd finally had enough, I turned it off and considered what to listen to next.

'Feel better?' asked Cat.

'Much better,' I smiled.

'Can I borrow this book?' She held up *Wuthering Heights*.

'Sure.'

'Well, I guess I'd better get going,' she said. 'My mum'll go mad if I'm not back by half past eight.'

She headed for the door.

'Cat!'

'Yeah?'

'You won't say anything to anyone will you?'

'I promise.'

Twelve

Cat was as good as her word. I just avoided my parents for a while, which wasn't difficult. Liam still occasionally pulled Cat's hair down. She still wouldn't believe me that he fancied her. Why else does someone like Liam do that? Ashok and Lenny said 'Hey' a few more times as we passed them in the hall between classes, but that was about as close as we got to a conversation with them. Each time, Cat waited until we had got far enough away before she let out a kind of squeal. I never let on that I fancied Ashok like mad. My smouldering eyes trick wasn't working anyway.

Then one day when I was singing in the loo, Miss O'Neill heard me. It was a small tucked-away loo, near Miss O'Neill's class and hardly anyone used it so it was perfect for a song or two when no one else was there. There was such great reverb. Anyway, I hadn't heard Miss O'Neill come and slip into a cubicle. I was singing a few verses of 'Summertime' before our afternoon classes started. I just love those lines which go:

'One of these mornings you're going to rise up singing,
Then you'll spread your wings and you'll take to the sky.'

They lifted me into the air and made me think I could soar into the future. Anyway, there was this clapping, the door to one of the cubicles opened and out came Miss O'Neill. Well, you can guess what happened to my face.

I quickly splashed cold water all over it, muttering and stuttering about being sorry.

'On the contrary!' she said. 'I enjoyed that. You're a really good singer, Flower.'

That made me even more embarrassed. But sort of good embarrassed.

'You would be great in our singing group! Why don't you come and join us?'

'I don't really have time,' I mumbled. 'I've got lots of homework and other stuff to do.'

'You could sing "Summertime".'

'That's OK.'

'Meaning?'

'Uh, no thanks.'

'Well if you ever decide to reconsider, it would be great to have you. Tuesdays and Thursdays.'

Miss O'Neill left and the door swung behind her. It sort of hesitated just before it finally closed. I felt a bit like that door. But Tuesday was my Mick day – the day he gave me flowers, and more recently the day when I went up to his flat which overlooked the flower stall to listen to his collection.

It might seem weird, a teenage girl going into this old guy's flat, but it all started because of Mrs Bhat who ran the newsagent by the flower stall. She kept telling me about Mick's music collection. She was pretty impressed by it. Finally she insisted that we all go up together. So she and Mick and I went up to his little flat. She was right. It was impressive.

He had this room with a sort of kitchen bit along one side and then two walls full of CDs, tapes and records!

Vinyl records! It seemed like there were millions of them! We all sat around and listened to music. It was quaint.

Anyway that was the beginning of my regular Tuesday visits. Sometimes when Mrs Bhat could get away from her shop, she would come up and listen with us.

I had never really listened to vinyl before. Sure, I'd been to discos where a kid with spiky hair brought his turntable along and mixed and scratched a bit, but I'd never actually sat down and listened to a record.

Mick would very carefully take a record out of its sleeve and hold it by its edges so that his fingers never touched the playing surface. I bet a finger had never, ever touched any of his records! I wouldn't have dared to take one out of its sleeve myself. He would lower it onto the turntable, turn a sort of dial that would send the record spinning at $33\frac{1}{3}$ rpms, then gently lower the needle onto the outside edge of the record. That was the bit that scared me. Putting that needle down. But Mick touched down in exactly the right spot every time. Then he would sit back with a little smile on his face and say, 'See how you like this.'

Sometimes I didn't like some of the tracks that much, but I didn't usually tell Mick that. I waited until I heard a song I really liked, and then I could get all excited about it. I loved Billie Holiday singing 'Summertime'. On the recording Mick had, her voice sounded further away than normally, but the words poured out of her so sweetly. I guess that's what her voice had. This sweetness – but smokiness at the same time, especially in the up-close recordings where you felt like she was right there. And sometimes it sounded like there was a car driving over a gravel drive in the background. Mick said the recordings were really old and made on old-fashioned recording equipment. I liked some of those old sounding records.

The other night, he got out someone called Nina Simone.

'Her voice isn't to everybody's taste,' he said, 'but you see what you think.'

Funny thing is, when Mick plays me something, we just sit there and listen. I look out of the window usually. And it's weird. It's so comfortable. We don't have to talk to one another.

Nina Simone was strange at first. I liked the slower, melancholy songs. Like 'Wild is the Wind' (despite the warbles) and 'Do What You Wanna Do'. And the other funny thing is, that even though I've never had a boyfriend, or even a romantic time with a guy, some songs make you feel like you have. It's like you know what it is to be madly in love with someone, and to lose them. Strange.

Sometimes at the end of an album or a song, all I have to say is, 'I really like that,' and Mick says, 'I'll burn you a disc then.' The next Tuesday there would be a disc waiting for me to take home. Mick labels them and I take them back and decorate them – do my own CD covers. Sometimes I draw on them (but I'm crap at drawing) and sometimes I stick on photographs that I download at the library. My collection is getting pretty big.

Mick says that I have soul. I'm not sure what he means, but it sounds good.

Thirteen

'Don't you think it's a bit weird to be going with that old guy?' asked Cat one Wednesday morning after I'd been to Mick's the night before.

'Why?'

'He's kind of old.'

'We listen to music. He's like a grandfather.'

'But he gives you flowers. It's a bit creepy.'

'Why don't you come with me?' I said. 'He's got this really cool place with more music than I've ever seen before.'

I didn't really want Cat to come. I loved having Mick all to myself but I felt she should get to know him so she wouldn't say stuff like that. You want people you care about to like one another.

'It's not really my idea of fun. Sitting around with some old bloke listening to old-time music.'

'It's not old-time music,' I said.

'It's not exactly "now".'

'It's classic stuff. You like Bella Armstrong. She'll be classic.'

'But she's only twenty-two. Most of them are dead!'

'So what? They've got great voices. They've got soul.'

I remembered that Mick had said that I had soul.

'I just don't want to spend my time listening to them.'

'Yeah. You'd rather listen to crap boy bands like all the other teenyboppers of the world.'

'And you're sophisticated?'

'I don't listen to crap boy bands. One-hit wonders who couldn't sing or play if their life depended on it. The only thing they've got going for them is that they wear the right hair gel.'

'So are you saying "Mint" are a one-hit boy band?'

'Yeah.' I rolled my eyes in my best expression of mild disgust. They weren't worth getting *really* disgusted about.

'Fake bad boys,' I added. 'The worst kind.'

'They're more popular than your dead divas.'

'So when has popularity been the measure of worth?'

'I think they're good.'

'To each his own.'

I thought maybe it would end there with my offer to agree to disagree, while implying that Cat had crap taste. Cat was not the sort of person who takes that kind of thing lying down.

'What's that supposed to mean?'

'Just what I said.'

'At least I don't hang around with perverted old guys.'

Now I don't mind arguing about music, or disagreeing about which TV show is better, but it got me that Cat was having a go at Mick. He was my friend. She had no right.

'You don't even know him,' I said.

'And I don't want to,' she shot back.

'He's better than you are any day.'

I knew as soon as I said that, it was a stupid thing to say. I was just so cross with Cat for being mean about Mick.

'Well then, you can spend *all* your time with him!'

cried Cat. And she stomped off towards Miss O'Neill's class.

'At least he knows good music when he hears it!' I shouted after her. As if that was going to pierce her heart.

When we got to class, Cat, who usually sat next to me, had moved to another desk. Liam sat down in the desk next to me.

'What's up, Weed? Why's Cat sitting over there?' he said.

'Why don't you go and ask her? Maybe she'll be your girlfriend now.'

'Oh. Lovers' tiff, huh?'

'Actually, it's none of your business.' I tried to get the maximum amount of sneer into my voice.

'Flower and Liam – when you are finished talking I would like the class to partner up. We are going to improvise characters from the novel we're reading.'

Oh great. Just what I needed. I sneaked a look at Cat but she and Tamsin were already partnered up. It seemed that Kerry was off sick. Tamsin had this sickly bright smile on her face and she gave me this really gloaty look. Cat refused to look my way.

'Looks like you're stuck with me, Weed,' smiled Liam.

It was true. Everyone else had partners. I was well and truly stuck with Liam. It didn't help that our improvisation was supposed to be an encounter between a girl and boy who have both lost the same thing and they both come across it at the same time.

Aside from the fact that getting up in front of the class and performing was my idea of Hell, I'd never felt less like being funny, which is what everybody expected with these things. Cat was really good at this and she could get up there and everyone would laugh and clap. I just felt mortified. Liam tried. In fact he pulled off his side of the partnership pretty well. I spluttered and stuttered and was totally useless. And once again the heat hit my face big time. Miss O'Neill finally put me out my misery.

'Valiant effort!' she said, cutting short one of my silences.

I managed to bumble back to my desk with the silence roaring in my ears. Liam on the other hand took a dramatic bow.

'Thank you. Thank you, everyone, for that wonderful applause,' he said.

At which point everyone clapped.

It was Cat and Tamsin's turn next. Cat of course was great. Huge applause and triumphant smile. I felt even more of a loser. Why I had ever said that to Cat? If I hadn't, she wouldn't have stomped off and we would still be friends. How could I get her back?

Just as I was going out of the door of English class, Miss O'Neill stopped me.

'Flower, can I have a word?'

Oh God. Was Miss O'Neill going to tell me off for being such a crap improviser? I didn't really want to stop and talk. I could see Cat ahead of me, walking with tedious Tamsin. Cat was laughing and talking like Tamsin was her best friend.

'Why so glum?' she asked.

'I'm not,' I lied.

'I know I've talked to you about this before, but I'm

trying again. You have such a great voice, it would be a real asset to our singing group. We have another practice tomorrow night and I would really love it if you would join us.'

Out of the corner of my eye, I saw Cat disappear around the corner. She tossed her hair and laughed. Well, I'll show her.

'OK, I'll come!' I said.

'That's great. I think your voice needs to be shared. See you after school.'

Fourteen

But I didn't go. When school finished all I wanted to do was get away. All day I had felt like a grapefruit that had been dropped from a high building. Squashed and sour. I sat alone at lunch and ate my stale cheese sandwiches. Even the lettuce was limp. My apple was wrinkled. If Cat had been sitting with me, we would have had a laugh about it – at the way my mother never seemed to notice when she left the crust on my cheese or that the yoghurt was past its sell-by date.

Cat avoided me and flaunted her new-found deep friendship with Tamsin. I took some comfort in the fact that she laughed just a little too hard and talked just a little too much for it to be real. I was hanging on to the hope that she was trying to get at me.

I was pretty glad when the last bell rang and I could escape. Cat hung out by the school gates with guess who. I got away as quickly as I could and hurried over to the library. At least I had my tigers.

Erin had sent me a new photograph of a Siberian with a cub. The cub was so cute! They make you just want to cuddle them so much. I felt like diving right into that picture. Needless to say the mother would rip me to pieces if I tried to cuddle her cub. I emailed Erin to thank her for the picture and checked out the news on the Amur Tiger Project site.

It made me cry. Another Siberian had been killed for

its pelt, its teeth, its bone – pretty well everything. A man was caught trying to smuggle the pelt out of Russia and he eventually led them to the scene of the kill. It turned out to be Tasya, a tiger I knew. She had a radio collar and for years I had followed the reports about what she was up to. When she was killed, she had two cubs, Borya and Tashi, who were just about to leave and fend for themselves. There had been a photograph of all of them on the web. I'd printed it. It was on my bedroom wall. She was such a beautiful cat. So huge, so proud, so strong, but not strong enough to evade the poachers. I felt like someone I knew had died. I wondered if the cubs would survive.

Fifteen

I sat out under the big oak tree in the field near our flat. There was a place where the trunk formed a niche you could nestle into. It felt sort of like the tree was wrapping itself around you. I liked it there. It faced away from the flats and you could look across to a line of hills which rose above the valley. You felt like you were the only person in the world. Which was good sometimes. Today it felt very lonely. The clouds were low and every once in a while the breeze riffled the leaves above my head. They were starting to turn brown. That somehow made it feel even more lonely. So I sat and sang. Sad songs, because that was how I felt. I sang a lot of them, some over and over. After a while I began to feel a little better.

Eventually it began to get dark. I didn't really want to go home because I knew my parents were there tonight and I didn't want to have to be with them, to feel like even more of an outsider. But I was hungry and my bum was getting sore. As I turned homewards, I ran my hand along the trunk of the tree. I always did. It was my way of saying goodbye to it. Suddenly I felt human flesh.

I screamed!

As I leaped backwards, I caught sight of a familiar mop of rusty hair.

'What are you doing here?' I cried. I was angry. Not only had Liam scared me to death but he was invading my very special place.

'You're a great singer,' he smiled.

'How long have you been spying on me?'

'I'm not spying on you. I come out here all the time.'

'I've never seen you before.'

'Unlucky, I guess,' said Liam.

I glared at him with the most glaring look I could muster and started to walk towards home.

Liam caught up with me.

'Go away!' I said.

'But I'm going this way,' he said. 'I've got to get back for tea.'

We walked on in silence. All I could think about was the fact that my tree was no longer my own. Liam knew about it. Now whenever I went there, he might pop up. I could have cried.

'You really *are* a good singer, Weed.'

'What do you know about it?' I said. In fact, I was flattered by Liam's words. That was two people who had said I was a good singer. Miss O'Neill and Liam.

He walked all the way back with me. Neither of us said another word until we got to my front door. I walked up the path.

''Bye,' I said.

'See you tomorrow,' said Liam.

Sixteen

Days went by. Cat formed a threesome with Tamsin and
Kerry. They were always forming little huddles between
classes. Tamsin and Kerry would squeal at some
outrageous remark of Cat's. Pathetic. I sat by myself at
lunch. It's lonely eating lunch by yourself in the canteen
where everybody can see that you're on your own, so I
started to go outside and eat my sandwiches wandering
around the school grounds. Even Miss O'Neill was cool
towards me. I figured it was because I didn't come to her
singing group that night. Liam didn't come out to the
oak tree again – at least not when I was there. I had stayed
away for a few days, thinking that he might show up, but
I missed that tree, so I went back. I was nervous the first
few times, but he never showed up so I got back into the
habit of going out there and singing my loneliness away.

And there was always Tuesday with Mick. I couldn't
wait for the bell to go on Tuesdays. I would rush over to
the flower stall and there he would be, with his bouquet of
freesias. I would bury my face in their strong, sweet smell
and then help him wheel the stall down the alley into Mrs
Bhat's little yard where he stored it all overnight.

'Time for that cup of tea,' he would say as he turned
the key on the padlock. He always bought scones from
the bakery and up we would go into his tiny flat. He
insisted that we have our cup of tea and scones before we
put on any music. Then he would wash his hands so that

he wouldn't get any grease or anything on a record. I washed mine as well, because now I was allowed to put records on the turntable. I was really nervous at first, but Mick had been so confident that I could do it without damaging them, I had to give it a try. And so far so good. I loved that ritual! The first soft bump of sound as the needle touched down, and then it floated along the grooves until it picked up the notes of the first song. I especially liked it if there was a little warp in the record. The needle would rise and fall in rhythm with the warp. Sometimes it would fit the rhythm of the song. At least it seemed to, but I suspect your brain has ways of matching them up more than they really are.

Billie Holiday was Mick's favourite singer. She was my favourite too. When we listened to her records, we both got into this kind of strange state. It wasn't a trance, but it was a world — and we were both in it. I liked it there. It was exciting and comfortable at the same time. I got so I could sing a lot of her songs off by heart and sometimes I would forget and sing them when we were getting our tea. When I realised what I was doing, Mick would say, 'Don't stop. That's ambrosia to my ears.'

We also loved Janis Joplin. I liked her more than Mick liked her. I would like to be as gutsy as her singing. If I could sing like that! When she sings those lyrics. It's so defiant. A challenge. And yet she's so vulnerable. It makes me want to cry and shout at the same time.

I asked my parents to bring back the old records they picked up with all the other junk. They thought I was crazy, but they brought them back anyway. When I got all excited about finding a copy of Janis's *Pearl* album, they asked me why I was interested in that stuff. When I tried to explain about Mick, they got distracted remembering the concerts they used to go and see. They were really into those terrible eighties bands. So I didn't really get a chance to tell them about Mick.

Mick has often said that I should bring them around to see his flower stall. I think they would like it, but it might make them sad, reminding them how they had lost their own flower shop.

Anyway, I really liked having Mick to myself. Mick and Billie and Janis and the others.

Seventeen

One day after school, I was in the library – excuse me, in 'The Knowledge Store' – checking out my website, updating it and answering various queries. Little kids sometimes asked the stupidest questions, like: 'I want to buy a tiger. Owr pet shop duznt sell tigers. Do you now where I can by one?' or 'I was in the park the other day and I think I saw a tiger in the bushes. What is the best way of catching a tiger?' Sometimes, it's just older kids taking the piss. When I finished up answering everything, I posted up a reminder about a film that night on TV about Siberians, and I was just about to close down, when an email dropped into my mailbox.

'Therz a sho on TV 2nite. *Panthera tigris altaica*. R u gonna watch it?'

It was from Cat.

I felt my face go hot. What was she up to? She might be watching me. Sitting with Tamsin and Kerry ready to burst into giggles when I looked up to see if she was there.

I tried swivelling my eyes around without moving my head. I couldn't see her. Even if she was serious and not taking the piss, I wasn't going to answer her and give her the satisfaction of thinking she could just email her way back into my life. But really, I would have loved to sit on the sofa with Cat and watch it.

I saved her email, but I didn't answer it. As I got up

to go, I had a good look around the computer area and she definitely wasn't there. I pushed against the exit barrier. I would go and hang out at the Bass Clef and listen to CDs. There was supposed to be this new female blues singer I wanted to listen to. Maybe they had her CD at a listening post. There I could forget about Cat's email.

I now knew every shop, every crack in the pavement, along the route from the library to the music shop. I had walked this way so many times. I was beginning to feel at home in this town. I stopped to look in the window of TKS. They had these great T-shirts with just a little bit of lace and sparkle on them. And some really good baggy jeans. All jeans were baggy on me, but these were cool baggy. I would wear a T-shirt like that and those jeans when I went on stage.

'Did you get my email?'

I was jolted back into the present. Cat's reflection appeared next to mine in the shop window. She was very close to me. I didn't dare look her in the face. I spoke to her reflection.

'Uh . . . yeah. Yeah. I got it.'

'Well. Are you going to watch it?'

She acted like the last few weeks of total freeze-out, silence, dropped friendship had never happened.

'Probably.' As if I would miss it for anything. I had been looking forward to this programme all week.

'Do you want to watch it together?'

I didn't answer for moment.

'What about Tamsin and Kerry?' I said.

'They're stupid!' said Cat. 'They haven't got a brain cell

between them.' She looped her arm through mine and started to walk me down the street.

'Where are you going?' she said. I could feel myself being swept along by Cat.

'The Bass Clef,' I said.

'No change there,' she smiled.

'I want to listen to a new CD.'

'I'll come with you,' she said.

We walked along in silence for a minute.

'Guess who I spoke to last night for five whole minutes at the corner shop?' said Cat.

It was the same old Cat. With the same old concerns. I felt myself smiling.

'Does he have curly dark hair, chocolate eyes and his name begin with "A"?'

Cat squeezed my arm.

'How'd you guess? And guess what else? He likes cheese and onion crisps. He doesn't like salt and vinegar.'

I suddenly felt happy. I felt my tight, lonely heart loosen in Cat's giddy enthusiasm.

'Sounds like a deeply intellectual conversation,' I said.

She ignored my comment.

'He has Mr Giles for science. And you know how Mr Giles is a little deaf? Well, they do the same thing as we do in his class. They speak very quietly and then when he turns up his hearing aid, they talk really loudly.'

And she babbled blithely on.

'And in all this riveting conversation, he no doubt swore his undying love for you,' I said.

'He said he couldn't live without me.'

We laughed.

'Look!' she said and she pulled up her white school blouse. Cat's belly button was all red and crusty, but looping through the crustiness was a silver ring.

'You did it!' I cried.

'My mum doesn't know yet.'

'It looks, well, it looks great,' I said, a bit dubiously.

'It's a bit of mess right now, but at the piercing place, they said it would take a while for it to settle down.'

Cat slid her blouse back down.

'Well, Ashok won't be able to resist you now,' I teased. I wondered what I would have to do to get him to notice me.

When we got to the Bass Clef, I couldn't believe my luck. Some tracks from Bella Armstrong's new CD was on the listening posts.

'Cat! It's here. I can't believe it! Here! Take those head-phones. Let's have a listen.'

The first song was s-o-o-o incredible! It was called 'Faint Whiff of Spring' and it was all about coming out of winter and feeling the first stirrings of spring and how that made you feel. It seemed to fit into what was happening to Cat and me – coming back out of the cold into the warmth of our friendship. Cat really liked it too.

There were three more songs from Bella's CD that you could listen to. I wished they'd put them all on. They were great. Even better than her last album. She just got better and better. Especially her lyrics. You knew what she was talking about. It was like she knew you too. Knew what you were feeling. I wished I had enough money to buy the CD right there and then, but I would have to wait to wait until my birthday. It was coming up in a month.

I babbled on about Bella Armstrong and Cat and I went back to my place, ate some chips and watched the programme about Siberian tigers. It was bliss.

Eighteen

Life was great. Cat and I laughed about my mother's really awful lunches. Tamsin and Kerry stuck their tongues out at us behind our backs. Liam hung around us occasionally and one time we even formed a threesome in drama class. Cat and Liam managed to pull off a brilliant sketch while I sort of played the boring straight person.

Ashok and Lenny said, 'Hey! How's it goin'?' to us when we passed them in the school corridor. Positively verbose. I had seen Ashok outside of school with Sophie, a girl in Year 10. Cat said it wasn't serious. I had given up smouldering my eyes at him, but I didn't stop dreaming about him. I never told Cat about how much I fancied him. She always assumed Ashok was hers, even if it was in her dreams.

Tuesdays were still my Mick nights, but Cat didn't say anything about it. It was just understood that on Tuesday nights after school I went to see Mick. He said I should try to write my own songs.

So, on Saturday and Sunday mornings, when I sat out under the oak tree, I started to think up my own songs. Just scraps of things really. Words sort of floated down, swirled around a bit – like the autumn leaves out there – and into my head. I didn't tell anyone about them. Not even Mick.

My parents carried on being madly in love with one

another. I was too busy with Cat and other things to notice very much. But when my birthday loomed closer, I thought I should remind them of the fact that they had a daughter, and with me came a certain parental responsibility – to get me a birthday present. I still hadn't heard the new Bella Armstrong CD all the way through in one go.

Nineteen

My birthday was on a Friday. And it turned out that there was going to be a Battle of the Bands that night at the school. Ashok and Lenny's band was going to be playing. Cat was going to come to my place for dinner and then we were going together to hear the bands. I kept imagining a scene where in the middle of their set, Ashok would take the microphone and with those wonderful, curled-up lips he would say, 'Everybody! Tonight is a very special night.' He would pause, look in my direction and then smile. 'And I would like to dedicate this song to a very special girl. She knows who she is.' He would then mount the microphone back on the stand and launch into this really steamy song.

My parents said they would make sure there was a cake. I said I hope I didn't have to remind them how many candles were needed.

'Don't be silly, dear,' they laughed, winking at one another. 'How could we forget that?'

And they didn't forget. After school Cat and I hurried back to my place and there was a lemon cake from Grig's Bakery with fifteen candles on it, a CD shaped object wrapped in Christmas tissue paper, and a note: 'Happy Birthday Flower! We should be back by six o'clock. Money for Indian takeaway on the kitchen counter. Don't wait for us to open your present.' There was also a parcel addressed to me wrapped in brown paper that had been sent through the post.

'Here! Open mine first!' said Cat. She thrust a floppy shape wrapped in blue paper with silver sparkles all over it. She had written on it in silver sparkly pen: *To Flower, my best friend*.

When I saw that, I nearly cried. It was a present enough for me. I very carefully unstuck the Sellotape, trying to rip the wrapping paper as little as possible. I would keep it. There was a special place in my drawer where I was going to put it. I would keep those words forever.

'Oh, c'mon!' cried Cat.

But I wanted to savour it, make the process last. Like cutting up the last bit of chocolate into little bits and eating them one at a time. I pulled the last folds of paper away. It was the T-shirt I wanted from TKS's window.

'Oh, Cat! It's just what I wanted! It really is!'

I threw my arms around her and gave her a big kiss.

'So you really like it?' she laughed.

'You know I do. But I didn't think you would get it for me. It must have been so expensive.'

'My mum gave me some money.'

I took off my school blouse and slipped on the T-shirt. It was a little prickly where the sparkly bits were sewn on, but I didn't care. It was the coolest T-shirt I'd ever seen and now it was mine.

'That purply colour looks really good on you,' said Cat.

I wondered whether Ashok might think the same thing, but I kept my wondering inside my head.

'Well! Go on!' said Cat. 'Open the present from your parents!'

'I know what it is,' I said. 'Or what I hope it is.'

'They wouldn't get it wrong, would they?'

'Only one way to find out.'

'Just rip it off this time,' said Cat.

I pulled off the paper and glimpsed the word 'Bella'. But the shape and colouring of the lettering was just a little too familiar. I folded the tissue back over and put the CD down.

'What's the matter?' said Cat. 'It's Bella Armstrong.'

'It's Bella Armstrong all right,' I sighed. 'But it's the last one, which I already have.'

Cat pulled the CD out of the paper.

'I can't believe it,' she said. She put her arm around me. 'Never mind. You can exchange it for the new one.'

'I know,' I said. 'I just thought that for once . . .'

I couldn't finish the sentence. I know I was being babyish but I almost started to blubber.

'But look! You have this other parcel,' said Cat, doing her best to distract me. 'I wonder who it's from?'

Maybe it was from my aunt. My mother's sister. She sometimes sent me something on my birthday. It was very neatly wrapped. It said 'Fragile'. It was so stuck with brown sticky tape I had to get the scissors and cut down one edge. It was the shape of a box of chocolates, but it wasn't heavy enough to be chocolates. When I finally got the brown paper off, sure enough the box said 'Chocolate Treasure Chest' but if there were chocolates inside, they must be for someone seriously on a diet. It hardly weighed anything. I opened the box. A pressed freesia. Mick had remembered! I had told him when we first met when my birthday was but I hadn't mentioned it since. Underneath the freesia was white tissue paper. I unfolded it and inside was a CD – a really rare live recording of a Janis Joplin concert. We had known it existed, but we had never been able to track it down. There was a note: 'I found it.'

'Wow!' I gasped.

'What's so special about that?' asked Cat.

'It's a CD that's really hard to get hold of. I've been dying to hear it and Mick somehow got hold of one.'

'Well, we don't have time to listen to it,' declared Cat.

Cat was still scratchy when it came to Mick. I would listen to it later. On my own when I would have the chance to savour every note. It was so sweet of Mick.

'I'm starving,' she said. 'Let's go get the Indian.'

When we had got back and set out all the tinfoil containers with the warm, sweet smell of peshwari naans wafting through the kitchen, the phone rang.

'Flower, sweetie!' My mother's voice. 'We've been delayed with this house clearance. The owners came late with the key and we're only halfway through, so start without us.'

Stick a lemon in my mouth, I thought. They had done the same thing last year. They never made it home until really late. I'd been sitting there by myself all night. Waiting. Why did I care? Why did I bloody care? I wish I didn't. At least I had Cat this year.

'You know I'm going to the Battle of the Bands tonight at the school?' I said.

'When are you going out?'

'Seven o'clock.'

'Oh, honey. We're not going to be back in time to catch you before you leave. I'm so sorry. Your dad is too.

We'll have to wish you Happy Birthday now!'

'Whatever.'

'Oh, don't be like that, Flower. We can't help what's happened.'

I was silent at the end of the phone. Stubborn.

'Flower?'

'Oh . . . thanks for the CD.'

'Is it the one you wanted?'

'Almost.'

'Oh, good. Well, I'd better go now. See you later when you get back from your big night out. 'Bye.'

The phone clicked and the dull buzz of the dialling tone hit my ear. I put the phone down.

'They're going to be late,' I said to Cat. 'They can't make it.'

'Never mind,' said Cat.

'On my birthday!' I wailed.

Cat gave me a hug.

'C'mon,' she said. 'Look at all this Indian food!'

'Yeah . . . and now it's *all* for us!'

I forced a laugh.

Twenty

The big hall at school was already crammed full when Cat and I arrived. It was dark, with beams of coloured light roving across the floor. Occasionally they would slide across us. They made the hairs on my arms stand up – like for a moment I glimpsed what it was like to be in the spotlight. Nice fantasy. In reality, even with my new T-shirt on, I lacked that star quality. Destined for the shadows.

'C'mon,' said Cat. 'Let me buy you a drink for your birthday.'

She grabbed my hand and dragged me across to where they were selling soft drinks. The cans stood in big bins filled with crushed ice. Tamsin and Kerry were serving behind the bar.

'What do *you* want?' said Tamsin. She put on that stupid singsong voice that people do when they try to be snarky. Cat ignored it.

'Flower?' asked Cat.

'Uh . . . Coke, please.'

'Two Cokes,' said Cat.

Tamsin was really slow getting them. She pretended she couldn't find them in the ice. She whispered something to Kerry. Kerry giggled and stole a look at me.

I didn't care. I felt so good standing there with Cat, wearing my new T-shirt. I knew they were jealous and I really enjoyed it. A spotlight raked my shoulder. The sparkles on my T-shirt flashed. Cat handed me my can of Coke and a plastic cup. I smiled at Tamsin as we turned away.

We bumped our way through bodies towards the stage. Cat turned to make sure I was behind her and as she did, another body came in from the right and bumped hard into hers.

'Hey! You almost knocked my Coke out of my hand!' she cried.

A boy turned. It was Lenny. He had a new pierced earring through the corner of his eyebrow.

'Oh, hi!' said Cat.

'Hey!' said Lenny.

'When are you playing?' asked Cat.

'I think we're on second last,' he said.

'Good spot,' said Cat.

'Yeah. It's good.'

'I can't wait to hear you,' she smiled.

'Here, give me your cup,' he said.

Cat held out her cup. Lenny looked around and then pulled a little bottle out of his pocket.

'What's that?' asked Cat.

'Rum. You want some?'

'OK,' said Cat.

'Hold it down low.'

He poured some rum into Cat's Coke. As he bent his head down, I looked into the little forest of spikes that was his hair. I wondered how long it took him to do that.

'You want some?' he asked, turning to me.

'Uh, sure,' I said.

I held my cup out low.

He poured some rum into it. I lifted it and sniffed.

73

'Don't do that!' he hissed through his teeth.

The fumes made me want to cough.

'You'll have Mr Martin over here in no time. Then we'll all be out of here. Goodbye champion of the bands.'

'So you think you've got a good chance?' asked Cat.

'We're the best,' said Lenny.

'Well, good luck. And say "hi" to Ashok for me.'

'Sure thing,' said Lenny.

He wheeled away towards the stage.

How was it that some people were so confident? Lenny really believed that they would win. And if they didn't, he would think that the judges were stupid. What made some people able to be like that?

Cat took a sip of rum and giggled.

'It tastes awful.'

'I like it,' I smiled.

'Or do you just like the boy who gave it to you?'

'He's cute in a hedgehoggy sort of way,' I said. But nothing compared to Ashok, I added in a thought bubble.

'I wonder if he'll remember to tell Ashok that I said "hi",' said Cat.

'No, he'll forget,' said a voice.

Liam pushed into the space beside Cat. His red shaggy hair was hanging in front of his eyes. He kept flicking it away with these funny little tosses of the head.

'Get lost, Liam!' said Cat.

'You're so cruel,' said Liam.

He turned to me.

'Isn't she cruel?'

'You're a pest,' I said.

'Anyway, their band will win,' said Liam.

'You think so?' said Cat.

'They're good,' said Liam.

'Are you going up there?' I asked.

'Are you kidding?'

'Why not?'

'Liam's too shy,' mocked Cat.

'Your attention please, everyone!' The voice of Miss O'Neill burst through the darkness. Feedback whined briefly throughout the air. We all turned towards the stage.

Twenty-one

The word 'band' seemed pretty loosely defined as the first three numbers were two soloists. One was a guy who played the guitar and then a girl I recognised from Year 9 sang a pop song. She wasn't that good but I thought she was really brave. I clapped really hard when she finished. Nobody else did. She gave everyone a big smile and did a deep bow. That takes guts.

There was a beatbox guy who was really good. I just couldn't believe that he was making those sounds himself. I was sure he had a couple of friends with drums behind the curtain.

There was a great band called 'The Back Room'. Year 11 boys. A girl standing beside us who was friends with them told Cat and me that they had been playing together for three years. They were so tight. They played a song that sort of reminded me of Joy Division. Their lead singer was kind of swarthy, with black, black eyes. I could have listened to them all night but they were only allowed to play one song.

'Hey, they're good!' said Cat.

Her musical taste was improving. I liked to think it was my influence.

A whole slew of mediocre bands played before the intermission. One of them had a girl singer fronting the band. She was pretty good, but the band was crap.

At break time I went to get Cokes for Cat and me. While I was waiting in the queue, Miss O'Neill came past. She was wearing this really cool pair of dangly silver earrings with big fake jewels. Also she had a great T-shirt on. She didn't look like a teacher at all. It's always so weird seeing teachers outside the classroom. I like it, but there's also something not quite right. I'm never sure how to talk to them as human beings.

'Are you enjoying yourself, Flower?' she asked.

'Yeah. It's pretty good. I really liked "The Back Room" and the beatbox guy.'

'They're good, aren't they? Terry – the lead singer for The Back Room – comes to my group on Tuesdays and Thursdays. He's got a great voice. He sings solo as well. Plays his own acoustic guitar. Completely different stuff. He's really versatile.'

'I wish they could have played longer,' I said.

'Well, this night has been so popular, we're thinking of having another one next month, but it will be open to all sorts of musical performance. Not just bands.'

'Sounds good,' I said. I wished I could have said something more interesting, but it was hard talking to a teacher. Even one as nice as Miss O'Neill.

'Well, I must go and sort out the next half,' said Miss O'Neill. 'Hope you enjoy it as much.'

She disappeared into the crunch of bodies.

'What took you so long?' said Cat. 'Lenny was back with a top-up, but we didn't have any Cokes.'

'Thought you didn't like it,' I teased.

'I think I'm changing my mind,' she said. 'He poured a little into a cup for us. Want some?'

'Go on, then.'

It felt so daring putting rum in our Cokes. I felt like Ashok might just look at me differently when I smouldered my eyes at him. Maybe I should try it when he was on stage.

The first band was an all-girl band with two guitars and drums. They could really play, but they did a really bad song, one of those where the singing is all like sheer, chiffony fabric. All floaty. Horrible. Cat didn't like it either. We giggled and did imitations of them. A boy beside us laughed and said, 'Hey, you two should be up there. You're a lot better than they are!'

The next two bands were really, really bad. They could hardly play and one of the singers forgot the words. I felt for him, but it didn't change the fact that six months' more practice might help.

Finally it was Ashok and Lenny's turn. They took a while to set up Lenny's drums. Everyone started to get a bit antsy, but finally they were ready. There was this other guy in the band called BJ who played keyboards. I had never heard them play so I really didn't know what to expect. Ashok lifted his guitar strap over his head, onto his shoulder, and I thought I would faint. There was something about the way he did it, with this little smile towards the crowd. Talk about butterflies in your stomach. I felt like I had a whole flock of birds in there. For a moment I even imagined he looked at me.

Cat grabbed my hand.

'He's so gorgeous!' she squealed.

We pushed closer to the stage.

Ashok looked over at Lenny and BJ, gave a nod and

this big wailing sound came out his guitar. A beat later, they crashed in with a driving beat and that was it – for the next six minutes I couldn't stop my body from dancing. Ashok seemed to alternate between his voice and guitar. BJ was great on keyboards and even hedgehog Lenny was great. Cat and I seemed to move together. It was like the music hit us in the same way. It just got inside you and made you move. Then before we knew it, they had finished.

'More!' shouted Cat.

Lenny heard her and smiled in her direction.

I couldn't quite bring myself to shout. Maybe Ashok would accidentally look in my direction and then I would catch him in my smouldering eyes. But he didn't. However, I didn't see him giving anyone else a melting look.

Twenty-two

Arm in arm, Cat and I inched forward with the crowd pushing through the foyer of the school. I had this lovely, buzzy feeling filling up all the spaces in my body and my brain.

'What a great birthday!' I sighed.

'See!' smiled Cat. 'It didn't matter at all that your parents didn't get back in time.'

I had forgotten all about them, until Cat mentioned them.

'Hey!' said a voice beside us. We turned round, like a pair of trained seals.

'Hey! Congratulations!' cried Cat.

'Yeah! You guys were brilliant!' I said.

'Told you we'd win!' grinned Lenny.

His grin was so wide and beaming, it made you laugh.

'Nice to be so confident,' I said.

'Well, you have to believe in yourself,' said Lenny.

'Where's Ashok?' asked Cat.

'He had to go somewhere,' said Lenny. He held open the door for us to through.

'Which way are you going?' he asked.

'Up Drummond Road,' said Cat.

'I'll walk with you then,' said Lenny.

My buzzing body dropped a decibel or two. I'd really been looking forward to walking with Cat. Just the two us. Laughing and talking about everything that had happened tonight. It would have been a perfect end to my birthday.

'So you really liked us then?' he asked.

God! Why do boys have to have their egos continually massaged. We'd already told him they were great.

Cat swallowed the bait.

'Yeah, you were really, really good,' she said. 'Got any more of that rum?'

'No,' said Lenny. 'I took that off the top of my dad's rum bottle. If I took any more he might notice.'

I looped my arm through Cat's.

'Where do you live then?' I asked.

'About halfway along Drummond Road,' said Lenny.

Good, I thought to myself. At least we would lose him part way.

'"The Back Room" were pretty crap,' said Lenny.

'Yeah. Not as good as you,' said Cat.

I couldn't believe my ears. Cat had liked them an hour earlier.

'I thought they were good,' I said. And I almost added, 'And so did you Cat.' But I wasn't that mean.

'How long have you and Ashok been friends?' asked Cat.

So that was it. Cat was going to try and find out as much as she could about Ashok from Lenny.

'We met up in Year 7,' said Lenny. 'I had long hair then, and I had these headphones on which you couldn't see because of my hair. We were in Mr Giles' class and I guess I was bopping to the rhythm a bit. Ashok asked me what I was listening to. I handed him the headphones, but Mr Giles caught us and gave us both a detention after school. On the way home we listened to the stuff I had been playing and he really dug it. So that was it. Best friends ever since.'

He talked a lot more about how much they practised and how they were the best band in the town. Soon we were about three-quarters of the way down Drummond Road.

'I thought you said you lived half way down this road,' I said. I was really dying to talk to Cat without Lenny there.

'Yeah, but I don't want you two defenceless girls to have to walk home on your own.'

He moved in between us and looped his arms through ours. Oh great. He turned towards Cat.

'You ever go ice-skating at the Leisure Centre?'

She giggled.

'No way.'

'It's fun. Lots of us go up there on a Friday night. You should come sometime.'

'Maybe,' said Cat.

'I can show you how to skate,' said Lenny. 'And we're playing a gig there in two weeks. You could come as my special guest.'

Talk about steaming in there. Lenny wasn't wasting any time.

'What would that involve?' giggled Cat.

I couldn't believe it! She was starting to flirt with him. With Lenny! What about Ashok? It was Ashok we were crazy about.

'Why don't you come along and find out?' said Lenny.

This was starting to make me puke. Thank God we were coming up to my road. When we got to the corner where I turned off, I had to interrupt them to say good-bye.

'Oh . . . are we here already?' said Cat.

'Are you going to be OK getting home?' I asked Cat.

'I'll make sure she gets home,' said Lenny.

Cat giggled.

'See ya, Flower! I'll give you a ring tomorrow.'

As I turned to walk alone down the quiet of my street, I could hear Lenny's voice and Cat's laughter tumbling through the night air.

Twenty-three

'You can come too, Flower!' said Cat.

'Oh yeah! And watch you two drool over one another!'

It was a week later and Lenny had persuaded Cat to go skating with him. Not that it took much persuading. Cat had melted faster than an ice lolly on a hot day. All week long Lenny had suddenly appeared walking alongside us between classes and teased and flirted with Cat like crazy. She flirted back. It was like I wasn't even there.

'Maybe Lenny will have a friend with him,' said Cat. 'For you.'

'Like Ashok?'

Cat shrugged.

'Lenny says he's started to hang out with a girl from Highview.'

Suddenly, I felt like a big toad had landed in my gut. But this was stupid. I didn't even know Ashok. Anyhow, he would never be interested in a girl like me.

'I'm sure Lenny has other friends,' insisted Cat.

I didn't want to go out with a friend of Lenny's. I wanted Cat. I wanted Cat and me to spend Friday doing stuff on my tiger website after school, and then come back to my place to listen to music. We could get some fish and chips and eat them on the way home.

'I don't need you and Lenny to act as my dating agency,' I said.

At that moment, Lenny the Limpet appeared from a side corridor.

'Hey! I've got something for you!' he said to Cat. 'Close your eyes and open your mouth!'

She stopped in the middle of the corridor. She closed her eyes. Lenny pulled out a packet of Maltesers.

'Now open your mouth!'

He almost put his grubby fingers right inside Cat's mouth as he popped a Malteser in. I thought I was going to be sick. Cat closed her mouth.

'Oh yum!' she squealed.

'Your favourite!' smiled Lenny.

Your favourite! Maltesers were *our* favourite. Cat's and mine.

'Another!' cried Cat.

'Open your mouth then!'

Cat opened her mouth and they repeated the disgusting ritual.

Cat held her hand out for more. Lenny dropped a few more Maltesers onto her palm.

'Want some, Flower?' he asked over his shoulder.

'No thanks,' I said.

'Well, I gotta go,' said Lenny. 'Here! You keep these Cat. I've got to get across the quad to my next class.'

He started to hurry away, and then turned round and walked backwards facing Cat as he walked.

'See ya tonight. Seven thirty!'

He bumped into a gaggle of girls.

'Sorry!'

They all started to giggle.

He smiled back at Cat, waved and hurried away

down the corridor.

'Isn't he sweet?!' she sighed.

But I didn't answer as I suspected Cat didn't really expect a reply from me.

Twenty-four

That evening when I got home from doing stuff on my tiger website, my parents were especially annoying. My mum was popping bits of cheese into my father's mouth as they got supper ready. I mean, was this infantile feeding activity contagious? It was bad enough with Lenny and Cat, but my parents as well! Actually it was something I would expect from my parents, but from Cat...well...I guess a week is a long time in the love life of a teenager.

I managed to escape from the kitchen pretty quickly and spent the rest of Friday night listening to Billie and Bella. They are great company. Better than Cat. Some of their songs are so right, that you can't stop singing along to them. They make you feel good, by knowing how bad you feel.

I wished I could have gone over to see Mick. It would have been good to sit with him and listen to some music together. I always felt good with him. But Tuesday night was our night and I didn't feel I could go and ring on his bell late on a Friday.

I didn't see Cat for the rest of the weekend. During the day, she and Lenny went out shopping together and on Saturday night they went to see a film. So on Saturday, I went to the library. I hung out at the Bass Clef in the afternoon and then came home and listened to music and read. I lay on the floor in my room for hours and just soaked in the flow of words. Sometimes a little island would come along, like Janis Joplin's 'Mercedes Benz' song. You could sort of sit up and smile in a song like that. Eventually my mother came in and said, 'Flower! Are you still up? You should go to bed. Young people need their sleep!' As if she cared. I ignored her and she didn't come in again. I woke up in the middle of the night, still lying on the floor, with the light on and just the hissy sound of nothing playing in my earphones. I crawled into bed and tried not to wonder if Lenny had kissed Cat goodnight.

Twenty-five

Well, it turned out that Lenny *had* kissed Cat good night. For the next few days that was all she talked about. Now when Lenny loomed out of the moving masses between classes, he and Cat held hands and she brushed imaginary things off his face. At least they didn't repeat that nauseating trick with the Maltesers. At first I tried making comments like, 'Did you hear that new indie band on Touch Radio last night?' and then more desperately, 'Did you know that Mr Giles was caught smoking cannabis between classes?' Finally on Friday, I waited for Cat after school but she didn't show up, so I walked home alone.

I was dragging my feet past the Bass Clef when a voice behind me called out my name. I wheeled around. It was Mick. I had only ever seen him at his flower stall and in his flat. It was strange to see him out in the streets. He looked older. More frail. I waited for him and noticed that he was walking slowly, as if he was having to take care to stay upright.

'Are you all right?' I said.

'Fine!' he said. 'I'm fine! Just getting old,' he chuckled. He wasn't wearing his deerstalker hat, which made him almost look naked – the way people do who normally wear glasses and then they suddenly show up one day wearing contact lenses. They seem like a different person.

'Why aren't you at the flower stall?' I asked.

'Just been visiting the doctor,' said Mick. 'Nothing serious. He just insists on my coming in for an MOT every once in a while. Mrs Bhat's son is doing the stall for me.'

He stopped to catch his breath.

'And why are you looking so glum?' he asked.

'I'm not looking glum,' I said, smiling. It wasn't really a fake smile, because seeing Mick did make me feel better.

'Well, come with me along to the stall,' he said. 'I've got something for you.'

We walked along, discussing the Janis Joplin he had got me for my birthday. I had taken it over to his place on Tuesday so he could listen to it as he hadn't played it before he gave it to me. Didn't want to damage it, he said. We had listened to it right through and then we replayed tracks that we particularly liked. Again and again. It turned out our favourite tracks were the same. We sang a duet of our best bits as we walked down the street. Mick didn't have a bad voice for being so old and leathery. People thought we were crazy, but we didn't really care.

When we drew nearer to the stall, I could see two people who looked an awful lot like my parents looking at the flowers on Mick's stall.

'There's that lovely couple,' said Mick. 'Don't even know their names. They often come by the stall. Never buy anything. They just admire the flowers. Appreciate the rare ones. They know their stuff.'

He called out.

'Hello there!'

'Hello! Is that you, Flower!?'

'You know each other?' asked Mick.

'They're my parents,' I mumbled.

'Oh, now I get it!' beamed Mick. 'Your parents who had once owned a florist! Now it's all starting to make sense.'

'Mum. Dad. Mick is the flower man I mentioned who is into music.'

They looked at me in a dumb kind of way.

'Uh . . . never mind,' I said.

My mother leaned over the display.

'These irises are wonderful. And they look so good next to lilies. Where did you get such perfectly white ones?'

'Trade secret,' grinned Mick, putting his abandoned deerstalker back on his head. Now I had the old Mick back. With his hat, he was back to looking young and well, and full of life. He went over to the bucket full of irises, took out a bunch, wrapped some paper round the stems and handed them to my mother.

'Here!' he said. 'To celebrate the fact that you are the mother of this wonderful young woman here. You must be proud of her.'

Her eyebrows lifted quizzically – just like they say they do in books. Proud of what? But she smiled across at me, then turned to Mick.

'Thanks but . . . no . . . you musn't,' she resisted.

'Please! Nothing would give me greater pleasure,' said Mick.

Finally she took them.

'You're too kind,' she said.

And I could tell she meant it. She really loved flowers. I guess it must have really cut her up when she and Dad lost their flower shop. Maybe I could win her heart with flowers. Bring her a big bunch every week.

91

'Well, we'd better get going,' said my dad. 'We've got a sofa to deliver.'

'Thanks for the flowers, Mick,' said my mother. My dad put his arm around her.

''Bye, Flower! When will you be back?' she asked.

'Later.'

'See you later then!'

'They're lovely, your parents,' said Mick.

'No, they aren't,' I pouted.

'Kids never appreciate their parents,' smiled Mick.

'Well, my parents don't appreciate their kid,' I insisted. 'They're all over one another. They stare into one another's eyes like they're the only two people on earth!'

'They're still in love with one another. That's a change in this world. I loved my wife like that.'

'But what about your kids?'

'I loved them too.'

'But my parents ignore their kid.'

'Well, *that* is not good.'

'My aunt says they haven't grown up.'

'Sometimes people don't. They're afraid of that responsibility of being an adult so they hide in their youth. Remain teenagers. Maybe it helps them ignore things they've lost. Like their florist. Don't let it get to you, Flower.'

'But it does.'

'You have a whole wonderful life ahead of you – and you've got talent. Passion. They will carry you beyond your parents. And maybe they'll learn from you.'

Unlikely, I thought. But I didn't want to say that to Mick.

'But I have a surprise for you,' he said. 'Come with me.'

We climbed the stairs to his flat.

'I know I'm a little bit late with this,' he said as we climbed, 'but as we boring old farts say – "better late than never".'

He sat me down on the saggy old sofa.

'Close your eyes and don't open them until I say.'

I could hear him opening cupboard doors, lifting lids, and generally banging about.

'You aren't peeking, are you?' he said.

Then everything went quiet. I desperately wanted to peek, but all my life I had been one of those kids who never peeked. I don't know if I was afraid that some peek monster would be able to detect the slightest quiver of a look, or whether I just really loved the suspense. Anyway, I kept my eyes tightly shut until Mick said, 'Now open them!'

Mick stood in front of me holding out a chocolate cake blazing with candles.

'Happy Birthday, Flower!' he cried.

The cake was a bit lopsided. It looked like someone had lobbed a stone at one side and it had caved in, but Mick had filled it up with heaps of chocolate icing. He had written, in a slightly shaky hand with pink icing: *Flower Power*. It was a mess, but a lovely mess. And above it all, Mick's eyes were dancing with the reflection of fifteen candles.

We scoffed about half of it at one go while listening to Janis all over again.

Twenty-six

The next day was Saturday. The clouds crowded low above my head. It felt like I might have to crouch down to pass under them. It was the kind of day when Cat and I would go to the library and trawl through tiger websites for new stuff, download new pictures and then come back my room and paste them into a tiger scrapbook we had started. She would probably think that was infantile, now that she was going out with Lenny.

As it was, I had spent every day last week in the library by myself, going through all the websites, so I pretty well knew every new addition to every site there was. One good thing was that Borya and Tashi, the two Siberian cubs, had been tracked down. Each had gone their own way, searching for their own territory. I felt so sad that they had separated. One day Tashi would have her own cubs. For now, she was making her way alone. She was brave.

But today I couldn't face going to the library. Old Crabby was giving me funny looks, like asking me, 'Don't you have a life? Do you have to spend every second of your spare time here?'

I didn't want to go into town. I might bump into Cat and Lenny. Tonight was the night of Lenny and Ashok's gig at the Leisure Centre. I would really have liked to go. I really wanted to hear them play. That number they did at the school was s-o-o-o good.

I knew Ashok would never notice me, but I wanted

to watch him sing. He had this quality. It wasn't just that he was such a good singer. He was OK. Or that he could play the guitar really, really well. It was that you didn't want to take your eyes off him. He was gorgeous.

Anyway, I had to accept that I wouldn't be going to see them that night, and I found myself heading out towards the big, old oak tree. It was almost bare now. A few brown leaves, like dying words, clung to the big twisty branches. As I sat there in my usual place, the wind occasionally stirred them into a kind of dry, rustly whisper. Sort of sad. Like they were calling out to the world before they all got blown away and disappeared.

I sat there singing one of Bella's songs, but somehow, I started to stray into another tune – one which I was making up, with words that sort of welled up from somewhere. It was all about sitting there alone under that bare oak tree. But it wasn't all sad and depressed, because the more I made up the words, the better I felt. I sang it over lots of times to make sure I could remember all the words and get the tune right.

I decided to go home and write down the words.

As I got up I could feel this sort of filled-upness in my stomach. It was a bit like after you've eaten a really delicious piece of cake and think that you might be able to have some more. I turned towards town and almost bumped into Liam. All that wonderful cake feeling lumped into a tight ball.

'How long have you been there?' I demanded.

'I just got here,' he said.

'You better have.'

'What's the big deal?' he said. 'You always act like you own this place!'

'I just don't like you sneaking up on me like that.'

'So what's up with you and Cat?' he asked. 'She's always with Lenny.'

'So that's what's up with me and Cat,' I mimicked. Why did I even respond to that? It was none of Liam's business.

'So are you going to hear their band tonight?' he asked.

'I'm busy.'

'You should go,' urged Liam.

'I'm busy, I said.'

'But it's going to be great gig. They're good. Really good. You can't miss it. We can go together.'

Go with Liam? No way!

'I don't mean like go on a date,' said Liam. 'I mean just go over there together.'

I thought of Ashok. Gorgeous Ashok.

'C'mon, Weed. It'll be great.'

Of course I wanted to go. But why was Liam so keen that I go? Did it matter? I wavered.

'It's the gig of the year,' urged Liam.

'OK,' I said.

'Great! It's starts at half past eight. I'll come round to you at eight o'clock. OK?'

'Yeah.'

And I headed for home to write down the words to my song.

Twenty-seven

All the way to the Leisure Centre, Liam was really chatty. It was really annoying. I kept thinking about how I would run into Cat and she would make some comment about Liam being my 'date'. And I deliberately didn't wear the T-shirt Cat had given me, although I wanted to. I was beginning to regret coming at all. As we waited in the queue for our tickets, I saw some girls from our class. I'm sure they were giggling about Liam and me being there together. His shaggy hair was even shaggier. Kind of big. I think he had washed it for a change. I tried to stand apart from him in the queue, but it was pretty hard to pretend we weren't together when he kept talking to me.

It was better once we were inside. It was really crowded and there were kids from all over, from other schools and even from other nearby towns. You could get lost pretty easily. It meant that I might even manage to avoid Cat. Except I couldn't lose Liam. He stuck pretty close. We pushed our way through groups of kids all laughing and fooling around and found a place near the stage. Lenny and Ashok's band weren't scheduled to start for about fifteen minutes, so we had to just stand there and wait. Liam kept talking.

'Liam. Don't you ever shut up?' I finally asked.

'I like talking,' he said.

'Well, I don't,' I said.

'Sor-reee!' he said.

He looked hurt. Something I didn't think possible for Liam. I started to feel guilty. I was being a real cow. Suddenly his face lit up and he waved his hand and called out.

'Hey, Cat! Hi!'

At the side of the stage about ten meters away was Cat. Her black hair was all shiny and caught up in a fake jewel clip that let some of it tumble down. She was wearing make-up and looked about two years older than she had yesterday at school. I suddenly felt like a schoolgirl. She was watching Lenny sort out his drums on the stage.

'Liam!!' I hissed.

'We can at least say "hi"!' he protested.

Cat looked towards us, smiled and waved.

'Hi!'

Then she turned back towards Lenny and called out something to him which I couldn't hear. I felt my face swarm with heat. Now she knew I was here. With Liam. Why had I come?

But as soon as I saw Ashok climb up on the stage I knew. He did that same thing, putting his guitar strap over his shoulder. Swoon-making or what? Out of the corner of my eye I saw Cat smile up at him, but I don't think he noticed her. Look this way! I directed all my energy towards him. Look this way! As he began to tune up, he looked up and right, and just at the moment when our eyes would've have met—

'Look!' Liam jogged my elbow. 'Lenny's got a new drum on his set.'

Oh, thanks, Liam, for snatching away that magic

moment. That moment, that might have compensated for a whole evening of feeling like I was on my own with dumb Liam while everyone else was there having a good time with their friends.

But when they started playing, all that clogged feeling in my veins loosened. From the first guitar chords, to the final crash of the cymbals, we just moved with the music. And it was brilliant music. Even Lenny's drum solo was great. They did some covers, but they played some original material too.

'Bloody brilliant!' said Liam.

He smiled up at me and I couldn't help smiling back. I had even forgotten about Cat for a while. Until the very end when they went off stage and I saw her squeezing through the crowd and throwing her arms around Lenny. There were girls around Ashok, but it didn't look like any of them was 'with' him in the way that Cat was with Lenny. I could see him nodding his head and smiling amongst them. I wouldn't dare go over and talk to him.

The hall started to empty and a big space was opening up around Liam and me. Just the two of us standing there. Definitely time to go.

Outside, Liam was excited. He talked about this riff and that riff. We went over all the little details of the gig. Until he said,

'Do you want to go and get something to eat?'

I felt my veins tightening up again.

'Uh no. I've already eaten.'

'Just some chips,' said Liam.

But I knew the chip shop would be filled with kids from school.

'No thanks,' I said.

Twenty-eight

All that next week, the oak tree was like a magnet. Even though the weather was getting sort of cold, I just wanted to be alone out there. I went there every day after school – except for Tuesday of course when I went to see Mick. And when I was there, I sang. It made me feel better. I felt like I wasn't alone. It didn't stop the loneliness, but singing made me feel better. And I was making up my own songs. Really my own songs. They came up from somewhere inside which was me, but a 'me' which I hadn't yet found. And as I sang those words, I felt like I was discovering myself, or myself was discovering what it was like to be me. It's hard to explain. And my voice seemed to know, to be part of all this. It got stronger. It knew how to sing those words. I wondered if Billie Holiday had made up her own songs. Or maybe it's possible to be so in tune with someone else, they can write stuff that is really you. But I sure didn't have anyone around like that.

My parents were even a bit more preoccupied than usual. I think they were having business problems. They spent all their time huddled together discussing things. They didn't seem to be so involved in their mutual admiration society. Mutual worry, more like. That made the oak tree an even more attractive place, as the atmosphere in the house was a little bit tense.

Liam had gone back to being his usual annoying self,

although we could usually have a conversation about music and bands and singers. I told him about Janis Joplin, so he downloaded some of her stuff from the internet and really got off on it. I felt kind of chuffed by that.

I did feel guilty about neglecting my Save the Tiger website. I know it's ridiculous but you feel like maybe your favourite Siberians (Tashi and Borya were now my favourites) know that you're not keeping an eye on them in the usual way. I got really worried that something had happened to Tashi, and as soon as I could on Saturday morning, I hurried over to the library to check if she was all right. She had been sighted two days earlier, looking fine. I wondered if you could lull a tiger closer to you by singing, the same way they say you can with a seal.

Twenty-nine

The following Tuesday when I went to see Mick, he wasn't at his stall. It was open and Mrs. Bhat's son from the newsagent was keeping an eye on it. She came out to see me.

'Mick has gone in to get warmed up,' she said. 'He's got a cold. Not feeling too well. He asked me to tell you to go up.'

I climbed the narrow stairs and rang the bell to his flat. It took a while for Mick to open the door. When he appeared, he had a blanket over his shoulders and he looked pretty pale.

'Flower, pet. Come in. Just what I need to perk me up a bit.'

'What's the matter?'

'Bad cold. Doctor told me to take it easy, but I couldn't stay in bed all day, so I worked until about an hour ago. Felt a bit woozy, so here I am, in the warmth of my living room. Cup of tea?'

'I'll make it,' I said.

I warmed up some scones and Mick and I listened to Ella Fitzgerald.

'She's not got what Billie has,' said Mick. 'But I like some of her Cole Porter numbers.'

When I left, Mick seemed a lot better. On the way home, I bumped into Ashok. Literally. I was thinking about Mick and I just ploughed into him without seeing him.

'Hey!' he cried.

'Oh my God! I'm so sorry,' I apologised. 'I wasn't watching where I was going. Excuse me.'

I think I went on and on in this vein. I can't remember exactly.

'It's OK,' said Ashok. 'It's OK.'

He hurried away, desperate to escape from this lunatic who couldn't stop saying sorry. Why was I such a klutz? Why couldn't I have come up with some witty little line which would put myself down and make him laugh at the same time?

There was a still a bit of light left in the day, so I went out to the oak tree. Someone like Ashok would never know the me that sat out here. I consoled myself with one of my favourite songs that I'd made up. It was the one about that oak tree. And how it stood out there in the field. Strong. Alone. Through wind and rain. I was singing it for the third or fourth time, trying to make sure I got everything right about it. In the middle of a pause between lines, I thought I heard the strum of a guitar. Was I going crazy? Guitars playing in my head? It seemed to get louder as I sang. And strange. It worked really well with my song. Was I able to make up a guitar accompaniment and hear it at the same time? I stopped singing. The guitar carried on for a few seconds, then stopped. No way was that guitar in my head.

I went back to the second verse and began to sing. The guitar began again. I sang right through to the end of the third verse. I thought of Ashok. He was the only person I knew who could play the guitar so well.

I stood up and crept around the big trunk of the oak. I saw a foot. As I poked my head round further, I saw that the foot was attached to a person, sitting up against the tree with a guitar across his lap.

Thirty

'Liam!'

He looked up at me and grinned.

'I love that song,' he said.

'How dare you!' I cried.

Liam didn't say anything. He just grinned up at me like a maniac.

'I told you to stay away from here!' I said.

'It's not private property.'

'How long have you been coming here again and sneaking up on me?'

'About a week,' he said. 'I was walking by last week and you were so caught up singing, you didn't even notice when I came up on the other side of the tree. And you were singing this song. The tree song. It was great. So I came back the next day after school.'

'I hate you!' I cried.

'Whoa!' said Liam. 'What have I done that's so awful?'

'You, you—' I sputtered.

'I've listened to your brilliant singing,' interrupted Liam. 'You're really great. And you made me want to work out a guitar bit to go with that song.'

I wished Liam wasn't saying these nice things. It made it harder to be mad at him.

'And I think it's almost working. Let's try it again,' he said.

I couldn't believe Liam was saying this. I had this idea

of him and this didn't fit into the Liam who was talking now. Most of the time he was such a twerp. He sounded so much more confident out here.

'I didn't even know you played the guitar,' I lied.

'And who knows you can sing like that?' he said.

Mick knew. But he had never heard of one of my own songs. I wasn't sure about singing these songs to anyone. They were deep down private things. That's why Liam felt like such an intruder.

'These are *my* songs,' I said.

Liam strummed his guitar lightly, replaying some of the chords he had played earlier. I remembered how, for a moment, I had thought the guitar sounds were coming out of my head. How had he been able to work out a music that sounded like it belonged to *my* song?

He played a few more chords and then started playing properly. It sounded like it could be the opening. It was hard to resist the pulse of his playing. He looked up at me. I began to sing.

It was strange. So strange. To be singing this song with someone there. Someone who was seeing and hearing what you were. And he was seeing something about you that no one else had ever seen before. He knew this other part of you. And he was clicking into it. Playing his guitar.

I could feel Liam's playing winding round the words, sometimes lifting them above it, and then pulling them back into the flow. It made the words work better. It brought out what I was trying to say with them.

It was magic.

Thirty-one

The next day at school, I couldn't even look at Liam. Yesterday, after we had finished the song, I had just hurried away. I didn't even say goodbye. I had felt so flustered. Like washing flapping on a line. I felt like I was held on by a single peg and if it loosened, I would blow away like a half-dried shirt.

Now, I was worried that he would try and talk to me between classes, but he didn't. He seemed to be avoiding me as well. At lunch I sat alone and occasionally caught a glimpse of him out of the corner of my eye. He was sitting with Darren and Tony, two idiot boys from our class. Seeing him with them, reminded me of what an idiot Liam was a lot of the time. I relaxed a bit.

The last class of the day was RE. The RE teacher was away and Miss O'Neill was taking the class. We were doing workshops about 'respect'. I was dreading it, and it turned out to be even worse than I had anticipated. Miss O'Neill put us in 'random' pairs. I ended up with Liam. Again. So much for the 'randomness' aspect of it. Anyway, the idea was that you went around the classroom and each person in the pair had to say something that they liked, appreciated, admired etc. about the other person. Liam and I sat there with this big space between us. Neither of us looked at the other.

At first, people were being really jokey and stupid. Darren's partner was this well-endowed girl called Jasmine. He, of course, said he admired her big 'tits'. The usual snickers all around. Even Jasmine laughed. She was a good sport.

Miss O'Neill was pretty good at situations like this. She somehow managed to allow people a bit of silliness but then steamed in, and everyone settled down and started to do it properly. As she went round the circle, I was filled with an increasing sense of horror. I felt like my brain was on a rack being cranked tighter and tighter. It was bad enough having attention directed at you like this, but then to have Liam as your partner – having to talk about him and him talking about you. Every time one pair finished, we moved a bit further round the circle. Like the slow hand of a clock. Ticking towards that moment. Slowly. Inexorably.

Cat's partner was Kerry. She made up this bullshit about Kerry being this easy person to talk to, but she did it so convincingly, I wondered what she would have said if I was her partner? Finally, it was the turn of Tamsin and Tony, the pair next to us. I was aware that they were speaking sounds and that Miss O'Neill was saying something to them. But I couldn't string the sounds together into words and sentences to make sense. Then it was our turn.

The heat flamed up from under my shirt, up my neck and burned my cheeks. When people say they turned red to the roots of their hair, I know exactly what they mean. I mumbled something about Liam knowing some good bands and being able to talk to him about music stuff. Someone asked me to speak up, so I had to say it all over. The other students had become a complete blur.

I heard Miss O'Neill say,

'And Liam?'

'I admire Flower's brilliant voice and her song writing.' He said it so loudly and clearly.

I nearly died. Why did he have to say that? He had no right to tell the world about my singing.

'Idiot!' I hissed at him out of the side of my mouth.

I sat on my hands and looked hard at the floor. The bell rang. Release. Everyone leaped up and headed for the door. I was just about to snarl at Liam again when Miss O'Neill said,

'I'd like a word, Flower, before you leave. And you too, Liam.'

She must have heard me calling Liam an idiot. I would get a lecture about breaking the 'respect' code in the middle of a respect class.

When the class was almost emptied and I was collecting up my books, she came over.

'Are you going to sign up for the music night, Flower?'

The open mike night that Miss O'Neill had mentioned after the success of the Battle of the Bands, was coming up in a few weeks. I knew about it, but she didn't really think I would perform in it, did she?

'Uh, no,' I said.

'I was reminded of your talent just now when Liam mentioned your brilliant voice.'

I didn't say anything.

'And what about you, Liam? I hear you're a pretty

mean guitar player. Are you going to sign up?'

'I'm not sure,' he said.

'I wish you would. Both of you. If you've got talent, you should share it. So think about it.' She checked her watch.

'But I've got to go now. Meeting,' she said. 'And I mean it. Please think about it.'

She walked out of the room.

I followed her out without even glancing at Liam.

Thirty-two

I didn't go out to the oak tree. Liam might come out there. I wandered around town by myself. Everywhere people seemed to be with mates, with friends, in groups, in pairs. I was going to go to the Bass Clef, but as I walked past the window to get to the door, I saw Cat in there with Lenny. So I went to the library instead to see whether Borya and Tashi had been seen recently.

First I checked my website. There were lots of messages and I spent about an hour sorting them out. Erin had sent one to say that she would be keeping a low profile for the next few months because she had some music exams coming up that were really important and she had to spend a lot of time practising. I would miss her. She was as enthusiastic as I was about tigers and she always came up trumps with great pictures.

Finally, after I had sorted out my website, I went to the Amur Tiger Project website to see how the cubs were getting on. It was always sort of scary, because I worried that something might have happened to them. After Tasya was killed by poachers, I worried a lot about her cubs. I opened up the site. Phew! Tashi had been seen not far from the old hunting ground. Borya was fine too. There was even a new picture of Tashi which a ranger had taken. She was lying down after having lost her mother. She was a bit young to be going out on her own and they weren't sure she was ready. But she was doing really well.

111

She had roamed quite far to find her own territory but now she was successfully hunting in a remote area. It was safer there than near civilisation. The first snows would be falling there. I could imagine her stalking through the trees of the those great forests, bright and luminous with the moon falling on the newly fallen snow. All alone.

Thirty-three

When I got home that night, there was a big vase of white lilies on the kitchen table. My mother was making pasta — for the third time that week.

'Hi, Flower!' she said. 'You're just in time. Sit down and I'll call your father.'

We sat down with this great huge bunch of lilies taking up most of the space on the small square kitchen table where we ate.

'How do you like the flowers your father got for me?'

'Nice,' I said.

'Say it with flowers,' said my father.

'They must have expensive,' said my mother.

'That lovely old bloke, that friend of Flower's, gave me a little discount,' said my father. He winked one of those awful adult to child conspiratorial winks at me.

'And your mother's worth every penny,' he said.

By now I was so sick of couples admiring each other in my company I wanted to puke. Or run away. But I was hungry. So I stayed and didn't say anything. I must have looked kind of miserable.

'Are you all right, Flower?' asked my mother.

'No, I think I'm coming down with bubonic plague,' I said.

'No need to be sarcastic,' she said. She gave my father one of those looks that sort of said: What demon have we spawned here?

113

He just smiled and turned to me.

'Your friend, what's his name? The flower man?'

'Mick.'

'He was looking a bit frail this afternoon.'

'Frail?'

'Under the weather,' said my father. 'He was moving a bit slowly. He's usually so sprightly.'

'He had a bad cold,' I said.

'I suppose he's getting on,' said my father.

I'd never thought about Mick getting on. Or ageing. He was just old. Like old people are.

'He must be at least eighty,' said my father.

'Eighty! No way!' I said.

'So how old do you think he is?'

'I don't know.' I'd never really thought about how old Mick was. 'About sixty.'

My mother smiled.

'I remember when everyone over fifty-five looked the same.'

But eighty was ancient. Mick wasn't ancient. I was sure my father was wrong. And anyway, I wished he'd stop nosing in on *my* friend. Before you knew it, he would talking about *his* friend Mick.

I sucked in the last string of spaghetti.

'Can I be excused?' I asked.

I had to go through this silly ritual at every meal I had with my parents, when in fact, I was sure they couldn't wait to get rid of me.

'What do you do in that room of yours every night?' asked my mother.

'Nothing much,' I said.

'OK,' she said.

It was a relief to get away. About twenty minutes later, I heard the television go on. Good! It meant that I could sing without my parents hearing me. The sound of *The Big Challenge* drowned me out.

I sang a bit haphazardly at first and then I couldn't help coming back to the oak tree song. It had reached the point where it was really working. I sang it through a few more times, making little changes here and and there. I started to think that the song was missing something. I sang it over again. And again. Then I realised what it was. It was Liam's guitar playing.

Thirty-four

The next day was Saturday. My parents left early to go to a car-boot sale in a nearby town. They let me stay home as long as I cleaned the flat, which I did. Sort of. The carpet in the living room wasn't really that dirty so I couldn't see the need of lugging out the hoover. I cleaned the floor in the kitchen and it looked pretty good as long as you didn't look under the table. I got everything finished pretty quickly and headed out to the oak tree.

I snuggled down into my spot but it was a freezing cold day. The autumn was turning to winter. I started to sing. I had a new song sort of unwinding in my head and it was starting to take some shape, but after a while my bum was getting numb with cold. My fingers as well. I stood up and stamped my feet, but it was hard to sing and try not to freeze at the same time. I walked around the tree. There was no one else in sight. I guess it wasn't the sort of day that you would bring your guitar out into.

Walking around helped a bit. I belted out a few verses, but eventually I had to admit that it was just too cold. Nobody else in their right mind would be out hanging around a tree on a day like this. I pushed my hands into my pockets, leaned against the tree and sang a few verses of the tree song. And that was when I heard the guitar chords. I kept singing, but I found myself smiling. I guess I knew then, really, that I was glad that Liam had come out to the tree. I finished the song and walked round to the other side of the tree.

'Don't get bugged!' said Liam. 'I was coming out here anyway. You just got here first.'

'I'm not bugged,' I said.

'I still love that song,' he said.

'I've got some others,' I said.

'Do you feel like singing them?' said Liam.

'Maybe,' I said.

'I mean you don't have to,' said Liam.

'If you insist...'

And I sang my new song, the one that I had just been working on before Liam got there. It was about never staying in one place and how that made you feel: that idea that when you arrive somewhere, you already know that you will be leaving it. So everyone you meet, you know you will be saying goodbye to them. I think I must have been getting worried about my parents being so serious and whispering to one another. It often meant that things weren't working out and we would have to be moving on. I just wanted to stay in one place for a while. And they had promised that this time we would.

Liam listened. He watched me as I sang. It was strange, but I didn't feel that awful self-consciousness that normally came when someone looked at me that closely. He asked me to sing it again and this time he didn't look at me. He closed his eyes and I could sense his mind playing itself a rhythm of thoughts that were chords tuned into my singing the melody and words. I finished and without looking up, he strummed chords, and picked at the strings.

117

Then he looked up and said,

'Should we try it together?'

'OK.'

'I'll start and then you come in when you think,' said Liam.

He began to play. He picked out a tune on the strings and then there was a moment when it just felt right to start the words. And the same thing happened that had happened that other day when I sang the tree song and Liam had played. The words rode on the guitar chords, broke, were submerged by a riff and surfaced again. And all of it made the words work. Made my melody stronger. By the time we got to the end of the song, I couldn't help beaming at Liam. And this time I didn't run away.

'Hey!' I smiled.

Liam smiled back.

'That was good.'

He strummed the final chords again.

'So are you going to be moving again?' he said.

'I don't know.'

'You haven't been here very long.'

'I know.'

'Maybe when your parents hear this song, they'll decide to stay for a while.'

'They'll never hear this song,' I said.

'Why?'

''Cos I'll never sing it for them.'

'But it's a good way to let them know how you feel. It's pretty strong.'

'Like what am I supposed to do? Walk into the living

room, plant myself in front of them when they're watching TV and say, "Listen to this"?'

'You could sing it loudly in your room and they would overhear it.'

'My mum would just tell me to keep it down.'

Liam blew into his hands.

'It's freezing out here.'

I had forgotten about the cold.

Thirty-five

I went out to the oak tree the next day. I knew that Liam would be out there too. I sang him a few of my other songs. He just listened. He didn't try and play along, but he asked if I wouldn't mind if he recorded them onto an MP3 player so he could listen to them at home and work out the guitar part for them. I hesitated, but he promised that he wouldn't play them to anyone else. I made him cross his heart and hope to die. And so on Monday night after school he came out to the tree with his player and I sang into the little microphone. It was weird. I tried to pretend it wasn't there and I was singing to myself. And I made Liam promise once again not to let anyone else hear it.

Then just for fun, I sang a couple of Bella Armstrong songs which Liam knew as well. We kept getting stuck on one phrase. First I would muck it up. Then Liam would. It was a really warm evening for that time of year and we stayed until it was dark. The moon came up over the hills at the side of the valley and I think there must have been a little madness in the moonshine, because we started to do silly versions of some of Bella's songs.

Finally Liam said he would have to go or his parents would be coming out looking for him.

'What about you?' he asked. 'Won't your parents go mad if you come back too late?'

'They probably wouldn't notice,' I said.

'I wish I had your parents,' he said.

I shrugged. I knew that he didn't really mean that.

The next night I went to see Mick, but that week Liam and I met up at the oak tree every day after school. Most of the time we did songs together. Liam had worked out the guitar for another one of my songs. It was a bit strange because it was about yearning for this person who is so distant you know that you can never be with them but you can't stop yourself feeling like you do. I wrote it with Ashok in mind. So every time I sang it, I thought of Ashok. I felt a bit guilty about that. It wasn't like Liam was my boyfriend or that there was even a sliver of that kind of thing between us. We were just friends.

In fact it was a bit weird during school, because during that week Cat started walking with me from one class to another again. She didn't have lunch with me, because she always ate with Lenny and as soon as the bell rang at the end of the day, she was out of the door meeting up with Lenny. But we walked together in school — only it all felt kind of cool. Distant. We had stopped being really, really good friends in that way you are — shrieking and laughing about things that only you and the other person know. Shared secrets. Well, there was none of that. In some ways it was even harder being with her without all that.

And the other weird thing was that Liam and I didn't really talk to one another much in school. It was like our friendship was a totally out-of-school thing. I think he was really wary after I got so mad at him after the 'respect' workshop. And it just didn't feel right to be mates with Liam in school. In some ways I think I would be embarrassed if people thought that Liam and I were 'bosom buddies' as they say in old-fashioned books.

So I still sat on my own at lunch time. I had managed to persuade my mother to let me buy lunches so at least I didn't have to sit there with mouldy bread and hard cheese. But there's something really awful about eating by yourself when all around you people are laughing and talking together and you can remember being part of that and now you aren't. I just always made sure I had a book with me and kept my eyes down, glued to the page. I got through a lot of books during lunch times.

I don't even think Cat noticed that I was always on my own. She was just so taken up with Lenny. They reminded me of my parents. I guess I was doomed to always be the person on the outside.

Thirty-six

The next Tuesday I went to see Mick and he looked terrible. It was a freezing cold day and he looked like the cold had got in and pinched him from the inside. He was all puckered looking. I persuaded him to leave the stall for Mrs Bhat's son to look after and we went inside where I made him some tea and a hot scone.

'It's this damned cold,' he said, taking a sip from his cup of tea. 'Now let me think. Who can we listen to today?'

'Do you have a female singer who sings with a guitar player?' I asked.

Mick put his fingers together in front of his face and thought. Then a smile crossed his face.

'I think I may have something,' he said. 'It's not exactly what you're after, but there's a couple of acoustic numbers.'

'I'll get it,' I said. 'You stay sitting.'

'No, I'll get it,' insisted Mick.

'Who is it?'

Mick ignored me as he pulled himself out of the chair. He groaned a little as he crouched down on his haunches to go through the records on the lower shelves. He fingered his way through a series of album covers.

'Damn! I just remembered! It's only on CD.'

He got up but it took him a few moments to fully extend himself. It was like he was rusty and needed oiling to get going again. He walked slowly over to the CD shelves.

'Ah . . . Here we are!'

He took a CD, carefully opened the thin, flat case and with his fingertips took out the CD. He pushed a button and the CD tray opened. I knew then that Mick must be feeling pretty bad, because he had trouble getting the CD into the holder. Usually he slipped it in with an elegant, perfect movement – not quite as impressive as his dropping the needle onto a record, but pretty impressive. Finally it was in, and he pushed the button once again and the drawer slid closed.

'This is from the late eighties,' said Mick as he closed the drawer. 'There are only a few tracks where it is voice with only acoustic guitar. But the whole album is full of heart and emotion. Brilliant lyrics.'

Mick had programmed the CD player to play the acoustic tracks first. I listened. The woman's voice was so powerful, but so vulnerable at the same time. It was like the words came right out of her insides. Really strong, not all namby-pamby like some acoustic/voice songs. The next one was this strange gospel type song. It was almost scary.

Mick closed his eyes but I knew his ears were wide open – letting the music fill his head. He couldn't stop his foot beating the rhythm. But his shoulders sagged and his face was sort of crumpled. And yet, this was young music. It was also young *female* stuff. Lyrics about feelings that it was hard to put together with an older kind of man. Then I remembered him talking about his wife. She had died when she was only fifty-three and Mick was fifty-five. And when he talked about her, it seemed like he was still in love with her. They had been together since he was eighteen and she was sixteen. I just couldn't imagine that – Mick as teenager. And he married his sweetheart and they stayed together until she died. Mick had said he couldn't really fall in love like that again. He'd met lots of lovely ladies, he said, but they just couldn't replace his Molly. There was a small photograph of her on the table. And just as I thought about that photograph, Mick opened his eyes and they rested on Molly's picture. For a few minutes, he was so absorbed in it, I don't think he even remembered I was there.

The CD finished.

Mick waited for a little while without moving, letting the last bars sink in. No need to break the spell. Finally he pulled himself up by the arms of the chair.

'So what do you think of that?' he asked.

'Can we listen to it again?'

He smiled and reached over and pressed 'play' once again.

We listened to it all over again.

When it was over, I stood up first and crossed over to the CD player.

'You stay there,' I said. 'I'll put it away. I want to see the details on the CD cover. You haven't even told me who it is.'

I picked up the CD cover.

'You ever heard of them?' asked Mick.

'I don't think so,' I said. The CD was by the Eurythmics. The album was called *Savage*. It seemed to be made up of a woman and a man.

'You'll sing like that one day,' said Mick.

'Fat chance of that,' I said.

'That's where you're wrong. You also have a voice that comes from inside. From your heart. From your soul. And you could write songs as good as that.'

I put the CD back into its place.

'I've written some of my own songs,' I said, but I said it pretty quietly because I wasn't sure if it would sound like boasting, or like I wanted to inflict them on Mick.

Mick didn't say anything. I stared at the CD rack. Finally I turned towards him. He was smiling at me.

'Well, aren't you going to sing me a few bars at least?'

'Well . . .'

'The Diva of Don Valley can't tell me she writes songs now, and then just go away without singing one of them.'

I decided to do the one about moving all the time. I hadn't even thought of a title for it, but Mick wouldn't mind about that.

I sang the first few lines. It was a bit shaky but then I forgot about the fact that I was performing it and started to be in it, in the same way I was when I was out at the oak tree. I could feel it getting stronger. I could feel myself getting stronger and more sad as I sang. It was sort of pouring out of me and by the time I finished it, I was back in that anxiety about moving. I almost wished I hadn't sung it.

Mick didn't say anything. He just smiled at me and I could see the gap between his teeth.

Finally, he just shook his head.

'I've told you,' he said. 'You've got soul.'

126

Thirty-seven

'We should put our names down for Miss O'Neill's open mike music night,' said Liam one night when we were out at the tree. He had worked out a guitar part for a few more of my songs and we had been practising.

'What?!' I gasped. I really did gasp.

'Yeah! It's in a few weeks and there's still a few days to sign up,' said Liam.

'No way!' I said.

'Why not?'

'I can't get up in front of a crowd of people and perform.'

'Why not?'

'I just can't,' I said.

'But you're good!'

'Look, Liam. I'm not fishing for compliments.'

'*We're* good,' insisted Liam.

'Why don't you sign up then?'

'I said *we*,' said Liam. 'What works is the two of us together. On my own, I'm just another guitar player.'

'You're a brilliant guitar player,' I said.

'What's the use of being members of a mutual admiration society if we don't go out and do it in front of an audience.'

'You do what you want to in front of an audience. Just leave me out of it.' I shivered. It was getting dark.

'I couldn't do it on my own,' said Liam.

He looked kind of sad. I almost felt sorry for him.

'Anyway, I wouldn't *want* to do it on my own, but I would really like to do it with you.'

He strummed a little lament on his guitar.

'I need you.'

He was laying it on a little thick, but it was starting to get to me. I was beginning to feel really guilty.

'I'll think about it,' I said.

We didn't say anything as we walked back across the field. I think we had worn our own path out to the tree. As I followed behind Liam, I felt his suggestion send a hot spurt trickling through my head. It got bigger. It fizzed. Like a sparkler. I watched the streetlights ahead streak slightly with the up and down motion of walking.

We reached the gate. Liam held it open for me to pass through.

'Well, have you had a think?' he asked.

'About what?' I said. I knew that would drive him crazy.

'The music night!'

Liam closed the gate and turned around.

'OK,' I said.

'What?' said Liam.

'You heard me.'

Actually I had said OK really quietly and quickly, so Liam wouldn't hear. As if that would somehow bury the whole idea, and keep it alive at the same time. I didn't really know what I wanted. I wanted to do it and I didn't want to. Is that possible?

'So you'll do it!' cried Liam. 'We'll do it?'

'I said I would.'

I started to walk away. I didn't want Liam's enthusiasm to get the better of him so he would end up throwing his arms around me, or something stupid like that. He caught up with me.

'You promise you won't tell anyone?' I said.

'But Weed! We have to actually sign our names on that sheet.'

'Can't we do it sort of without anyone noticing? You know, at the very last minute, just as the notice is coming down, we put our names on it?'

Liam looked at me like I was crazy.

'Yeah, I guess,' he said.

'Let's do it that way then. Promise?'

'Promise,' said Liam.

He stuck his hands in his pockets.

'But now, I want you to come with me. I've got something to show you.'

'Where?'

'My house.'

'But it's late.'

'Your parents won't be home.'

Liam was right. They were getting home later and later. And I'd heard them talking about what it would be like to live in Wales. Beautiful hills. Getting in touch with old friends who lived in a really nice town in mid Wales. Reminding each other about that last time they had been there, before I was born, and what a good time they'd had. It was making me really nervous. They had promised we would stay here. And now they were talking about Wales. I shoved it all somewhere back with all the other rubbish in my head. I couldn't bear to think about it. I tried not to, but the worry beat beneath all the normal everydayness of everything.

'OK.'

I'd never been to Liam's house before. He lived just a few streets away from our place. I knew he had a younger sister who was still in primary school. And that he had lived in that house all his life.

But as we walked past the houses lighting up all yellow and warm-looking through their windows, I couldn't help thinking about what I'd let myself in for – singing in front of the whole school. Which song should we do? There was that Bella Armstrong one. Or that Eurythmics one that I had heard at Mick's. That was really good. I'd have to get a copy and we'd have to work on it. I started to get excited. Despite myself.

'Here we are,' said Liam, pushing open the gate in front of a small terraced house.

He rang the bell.

The door flew open and a small girl with a big bloom of flyaway blonde hair cried, 'Liam's home!'

'Well, I hardly thought it was the ghost of Christmas past!' shouted a woman's voice from inside.

'Hi, Mum!' called Liam.

'Hello, love! I'm in just in the middle of a calculation. I'll talk to you later.'

'I've got Flower with me to show her you-know-what.'

Flower? Liam never called me anything but Weed.

'Well, you know where your-know-what is.'

All this you-know-whatting was starting to get on my nerves, but I could tell that Liam was all gee'd up about you-know-what, whatever you-know-what was.

'Come on,' said Liam.

I followed him up the stairs. He opened a door, held it open for me and swept his arm towards the bed with a flourish.

'Da-da!'

A shiny, but slightly battered, red electric guitar lay across the bed.

'Is that yours?' I said.

Liam picked it up and struck a pose somewhere between Liam the geek and Jimi Hendrix. Ashok he was not. But he looked so proud.

'When did you get that?'

'Yesterday. I saved up money from my aunts and uncles from Christmases and birthdays and finally got enough for this beautiful second-hand axe.'

Somehow, Liam calling a guitar an axe sounded silly. On the other hand, it was really a nice-looking guitar.

He plugged it into an amp and started to tune it.

'Do your parents let you play it that loud?'

'I've got certain times when I can play. My mum puts up with it for awhile and then it starts to drive her crazy, but she lets me play.'

He played a few chords and then broke into the riff that began 'Movin''. He played the whole thing. It sounded great all electric.

'Do you think you could sing to that?'

I couldn't wait to give it a go.

'Let's try it!'

Thirty-eight

'But it's such a good song!'

It was lunch time a few days later and Liam had come to sit with me in the canteen. I was trying to convince him that we should do Bella's song as our number on the music night.

'I think we should do one of your songs.'

'Keep your voice down. Everyone will hear us.'

'Let's go outside, then,' said Liam,

We got up. I hoped no one had heard Liam refer to 'my' songs. We walked across the school grounds and we could see our breath in the cold wintry air.

'I do not want to do one of my songs.'

'Why not?'

'I don't want to.'

'You're scared.'

'You're right, I *am* scared.'

It was true. I didn't want to bare my soul in front of all those people. And for a moment, that straight answer shut Liam right up.

'Anyway, that Bella song is me. I feel that. I feel what she means.'

'But don't you want to have that effect on people too? Make that connection. Because that's what your song does.'

'It's too close to the bone.'

'It sounds so great.'

Liam said this like it was his last word on the subject

and I knew I had won. He wouldn't pursue it for at least another twenty-four hours.

He was right though. We had done an electric version of 'Movin'' (that was the title I had given my moving song) and it had given it a new powerful drive – it felt really vulnerable at the same time. But now, it was too close to the bone. Just like I said. Singing it touched that nerve and I got kind of heavy-hearted when I sang it.

Across the school grounds I saw Cat and Lenny. They were talking to Ashok and a girl from Year 9. I didn't want them to see me out here walking around with Liam.

'I've got to go and collect some books from my locker,' I said.

'I'll come with you,' said Liam.

'No. I've got to go to the loo,' I said. 'See you in class.'

And I hurried away.

Last class that afternoon Miss O'Neill announced that this afternoon was the last chance to sign up for the music night. The list was coming down at four o'clock and there were only a few places left. She knew of a couple of people who were still deciding, so whoever wanted to perform better get in quick. I knew Liam was going to look at me and give me that stare that would say, 'See what you've done? We might miss our chance now.' I avoided looking in his direction.

The last bell rang and I headed for the door. Liam caught up with me just as I was slipping into the hubbub in the corridor.

'We better hurry if we're going to make it into the music night. You heard what Miss O'Neill said,' said Liam.

'But if there are people who really do want to enter, then it's better that—'

'Weed, you said you would.'

'I know, but I didn't think it would be so popular. I thought we could get away without having to sign our names. Get in at the last minute.'

We were coming up to the notice board. Liam slowed down.

'Let's just think about it a minute,' and I pulled Liam past the notice. I could see that there were still two band places left.

At that moment Ashok came around the corner, and stopped in front of the notice board. He dug around inside his blazer pocket, pulled out a pen and started to write in one of the empty spaces.

'Damn!'

He looked around.

'Hey, have either of you got a pen? Mine's run out,' he called out to Liam and me.

'Uh, yeah,' I said.

I unzipped my pencil case. All the pens and pencils cascaded out, and rattled across the floor.

'Oh shit,' I cried.

'I only wanted one,' smiled Ashok.

He strolled over, picked up a ballpoint and returned to the notice. I watched him scribble on the paper while I scrabbled around trying to get all my pencils and stuff back into my case. Liam helped me.

'Are you all right?' Liam asked.

'Of course I'm all right,' I hissed.

Ashok strolled back, picked up a few strays we'd missed

134

and handed me back the pen.

Then he walked away.

One place left.

At that moment, Tamsin and Kerry came out of Miss O'Neill's class further down the hall. They headed towards us, a pen in Tamsin's hand. She had a smug smile on her face. I was about three metres from the notice board. She was about ten metres away and getting closer.

'C'mon, Weed!' said Liam.

Tamsin was almost there.

I felt my legs moving. One – two- three – four – five steps. I was in front of the notice. Tamsin was a metre away.

'How do you spell your last name, Liam?'

He beamed.

'P–u–s–h–a–r–s–k–i.'

I watched my hand write with a scratchy, slanty, unsteady line: 'Pusharski and Power (guitar and vocals)'. The letters wavered in front of my eyes. Now I'd done it. We were signed up.

Thirty-nine

Seeing Tamsin coming down the corridor intent on taking that last spot had made me realise how much I really wanted Liam and me to have it. At least that was what I thought at that moment.

Now, a few days later I was having second thoughts. Miss O'Neill had asked us all to tell us what we were going to perform and to do a vague rendition of it so she could schedule the acts to make the evening work. She didn't want things to clash or get too wearing – like all those male hormones in the heavy metal music that seemed to be dominating the evening. We were going to have to make a decision about what we were going to perform. Liam was still trying to persuade me to do 'Movin''. Miss O'Neill said she wanted all of us to stay after school the next night to do a quick run through of our numbers. We were supposed to meet her in the music room at four o'clock. She had guitars, drums, keyboards, playback machines and all sorts of stuff at our disposal.

I was walking back from school via Mick's trying to work out how to get out of it. I turned the corner, but Mick wasn't on the stall. Mrs Bhat's son was taking some money from a lady standing there with a big bunch of white flowers. Mick must be up in his flat. I headed towards the door.

'Flower!' Mrs Bhat's voice called from the doorway of her shop before I got there.

I turned round.

'Hi! Is Mick feeling rotten again?' I asked.

She came over to me.

'Oh, Flower. He was feeling very bad, and this morning the doctor sent him off to the hospital. Bad chest infection. The doctor said it was the only way he could make sure Mick would take care of himself and not sneak out here to sell his flowers.'

'Did you see him go? Was he really ill?'

'I drove him over. He seemed OK. He said if you have a chance, he would like very much if you came to visit.'

Mick in the hospital! I could never imagine Mick anywhere but at his flower stall and in his flat. When people say 'my heart thudded' – I suddenly really knew what it meant. I could feel mine in there pounding away. Then I remembered—

'Liquorice allsorts! I'll get him some liquorice allsorts. He loves those.'

Mrs Bhat and I went into her shop to get the allsorts. I tried to pay her, but she wouldn't accept any money. She gave me a huge box of them. It was another thing Mick and I shared, a love of liquorice allsorts.

The hospital wasn't that far away. It only took me about twenty minutes to get to the big glass doors that led into a large reception area. There was a group of nurses huddled by the door, smoking.

Inside, it was all new and modern, but it still smelled like a hospital. I used to like that smell when I was a kid and had to go to the hospital for a broken finger. It made me want to be a doctor. Now it sort of scared me. Or maybe it wasn't the smell that scared me. Maybe it was the fact that Mick was in here. Mrs Bhat had made it all sound routine, and I was sure she was right. But I didn't like the idea of Mick in a hospital.

I didn't even know if I was allowed in here. Were there rules about hours and who could come and visit someone? Did they have to be relatives? I'd never visited anyone in hospital before.

I must have looked kind of lost because a woman behind reception called out to me.

'Can I help you?'

'Uh, I hope so. I don't know. I've come to visit someone,' I said.

'Do you know what ward they're in?'

'No.'

'Name?'

At that moment, I realised that I didn't know Mick's last name. He was always just 'Mick' to me. If I didn't even know his last name, they might think I didn't really know him well enough to be let in to visit. I could feel myself getting red.

'Um, well, his name is Mick,' I stuttered.

'Last name?'

'Um . . . I don't know,' I said lamely.

'Well, who are you?'

'A friend.'

'Do you know why he's in?'

'Chest infection.'

'That's *some* help,' she said. 'When was he admitted?'

'This morning,' I said.

The receptionist ran a long pink fingernail down a column of names. Then down another column of names.

'Mick Flanagan?'

'I don't know.'

'Well, a Mick Flanagan was admitted today to Fleming Ward. Go up the stairs to the first floor and follow the blue lines on the floor until you get a set of double doors. Turn right. When you come to a crossroads, so to speak. Go left and second door on the left – that's Fleming Ward.'

The hospital corridors felt strangely empty. The only people I seemed to meet were old men in slippers and tartan bathrobes and women attached to those intravenous feeding bags which they pushed along beside them. I was so worried I was going to come across Mick being wheeled down the corridor on a trolley.

When I finally got to a door with a smart plexiglass sign above it saying 'Fleming Ward', I hovered outside. What if Mick wasn't in there? Or what if he was and he looked really ill and ghastly? And what if everyone turned to stare at me?

'Going in?' smiled a nurse as she pushed the door open for me.

And so I was swept into Fleming Ward.

At first all I could see was a row of grey hair down one side of the room. I couldn't make out one face from another. Then I heard a voice calling me from the other side of the room.

'Flower!'

And there was Mick, at the end of another row of beds. His was closest to the window. He was sitting up against a pile of pillows, pulling off a set of headphones. He didn't look ill at all. In fact he looked better than I had seen him in the last few weeks. I needn't have worried.

Forty

'Look! They've put me in here with a load of old men!' whispered Mick.

I looked along the other row of beds. Another line of grey grizzled heads with sagging jaws lay against the white pillows.

'Don't worry. They'll probably kick you out soon for being too young,' I giggled.

'And they wouldn't let me keep my hat on!'

Which exposed Mick's head, also grey and grizzled. But he was different. He wasn't one of them.

'It's so good to see you, Flower!'

'I've brought you something,' I said, and handed him the box of allsorts.

'Manna from heaven!' he beamed. 'Everything they say about hospital food is tr—'

Mick coughed. Followed by another and then a whole cascade of coughs that shook his whole body.

'Bloody cough,' he said, and opened the box.

'Now I suppose I should offer you first choice as you're my guest, but I know which ones you'll take.'

I laughed. Mick and I both liked the liquorice tubes with white filling the best.

'You go first. It's your present,' I said.

Mick picked out two of the liquorice tubes and handed me the box. I counted the liquorice tubes left.

'There are eleven left.'

'Well, I shall enjoy them!' he said.

'Minus two,' I said, picking out a few and popping one in my mouth.

'Now, don't you go eating all my favourites,' he said.

He dipped his hand in and took another.

But just as he was about to put it into his mouth he started coughing again. It seemed to go on for a long time. Finally he stopped.

'So how's the singing?' he asked.

This jolted me back to the current dilemma about our performance night.

'OK,' I demurred.

'So when are you cutting your first album?'

'Well... something *has* come up. There's a sort of performance night at the school and this friend of mine ... well, he plays the guitar.'

'And?'

'And... we... he and I... we're going to do a song together.'

'Flower! That's great! What are you going to do?'

'Well... that's the problem. I want to do a Bella Armstrong song – and he doesn't.'

'Why don't you do the song that you sang at my flat?'

'That's the one *he* wants to do.'

'Well, I'm on his side on this one,' said Mick. 'That song is you, Flower.'

'Yeah. I know.'

I smiled – weakly. Very weakly. I looked out of the window.

I could feel Mick studying my face. I could feel the pressure from him to do my own song.

'When is it happening?' he asked finally.

'Two weeks.'

'Would it be all right if I came?' asked Mick.

'Do bears shit in the forest?' I smiled. 'Will you be better by then?'

'I'm not going to miss your first public performance!' said Mick indignantly. He leaned back against the pillows. 'And I'm going to offer you an opinion – whether you like it or not. I think *you* have as much to say as Bella Armstrong.'

Forty-one

'Flower! Liam!' Miss O'Neill called out our names as Ashok and Lenny played the last few bars of their number. I looked for an abyss to jump into. It was bad enough that we had to play in the first place, but when I heard that Ashok was playing just before us, I wanted to run away. He would hear us! The only thing that kept me there was the ball and chain Liam had clamped on me. Not really, but he held me tight with a look like superglue. I had been through the hot sweats, the cold sweats. Still hadn't got anywhere near the 'No sweat' stage. I hadn't even been able to enjoy Ashok's playing, I was so stressed out.

It was really late. We had been waiting for hours, it seemed. There had been a fire alarm at the school – a false one and everyone had been evacuated, so by the time we all got back in, everything was running late. Miss O'Neill was stressed out big time as well.

Liam was just picking up his guitar when the caretaker poked his head in the door.

'Miss O'Neill. I'm afraid you're going to have to vacate this room. The evening class will be here any minute.'

'Is it that late already?' asked Miss O'Neill. 'Damn!'

'Flower... Liam,' she said, looking at us with lines crumpling up her forehead. 'I'm really sorry. We won't be able to hear you. But it says here that you're going to do a Bella Armstrong song – one that I'm familiar with.

I'll slot it in so that it fits into the greater scheme of things.'

'Actually,' said Liam. 'We're thinking of doing a different—'

'Miss O'Neill!' interrupted the caretaker. 'People are waiting to come in.'

Miss O'Neill jumped off the edge of the table where she was sitting with her clipboard.

'Don't worry. We're coming!'

'Miss O'Neill—' said Liam.

'I'll talk to you about it tomorrow, Liam. OK! Everyone out!'

I've never felt such a sense of relief – like a balloon that was about to burst, when someone releases that little bit you blow into, and all the air rushes out. I felt like zooming around the room the way a balloon does, too.

Out in the hall, Liam slung his guitar over his back.

'We've got to tell her we're doing "Movin'"' instead of the Bella Armstrong,' he said.

'I don't think we can change it now,' I protested.

'What do you mean?'

'She's got us down to play Bella. It's too late to change it.'

Liam just looked at me with that look of total exasperation that he has.

'I don't believe you,' he said. And he walked away down the corridor and out into the early darkness.

Forty-two

When I got home, I waited and then I rang Liam, but he wouldn't answer his phone. He must be really mad at me, because he's never not answered my calls before. I tried his landline. His mother answered.

'Hi, Flower. I'll just get him,' she said in her loud, enthusiastic voice.

I heard her calling him.

Eventually she came back on the line.

'He's right in the middle of doing something, Flower.'

That was all she said.

'Could you just tell him that I rang?' I said. He wouldn't talk to me. All because of a stupid song. *My* song. Why should he care what song we did? At least I had agreed to get up there and do a song with him. What more does he want? It's not as if *he's* baring his soul out there. It's easy for him.

My parents weren't back yet and they hadn't left a message or anything to say when supper would be. I could have cooked something for us, I guess. I can boil pasta as well as my mother and that's probably what we'd be having again. But I didn't want to stay in an empty house. I wanted to see Mick.

Mick was still in the hospital, but the doctor said he was recovering well and he could leave soon.

I dropped by Mick's flower stall on my way to the

hospital. Mrs Bhat was helping her son close up the stall at the end of the day. They were keeping it open while Mick was in hospital. The flowers were getting a bit bedraggled. No one could keep it like Mick did.

'How is he today?' she asked.

'I'm just on my way,' I replied. 'He was looking good yesterday. Should be back soon.'

'I think the doctor will keep him in to stop him from standing out here in the freezing cold,' said Mrs Bhat. 'He is so stubborn.'

'How much are the freesias?' I asked.

'Freesias?'

'Those white ones with the lovely smell.'

'The ones which Mick always gives to you?'

'Today I want to give some to him.'

'You don't have to pay,' said Mrs Bhat.

'I can't give Mick his own flowers as a present and not pay for them.'

I put two pounds on the counter and inhaled the sweetness of the freesias. Mrs Bhat had managed to get a fresh order of them. Mick would like these. They would fill his little corner of the room with the smell of home.

The woman on reception smiled at me. She was getting used to me seeing me now. I visited Mick every day. He was always sitting up waiting and as soon as I appeared, he would call out something silly like, 'Flower! You're here. The day has finally blossomed!'

Today I was later than usual because of the after-school auditions. Mick was slumped down into his pillow wearing his huge headphones which he insisted

I bring in from his flat. His eyes were closed. He was very still. I went over and stood by his bed. He didn't stir. I waited.

Suddenly he inhaled deeply, said, 'Freesias! Flower!' and opened his eyes. The gap between his teeth appeared. The big smile.

'These are for you,' I said.

'No. You should be taking them home. It's your day for freesias.'

'Today, it's *your* day for freesias.'

I got a vase from the collection on the windowsill.

'OK,' he whispered. 'It will help to cover up the smell of old men.'

I put them on the bedside table where Mick had a stack of CDs.

'So how did it go?' he asked.

'How did what go?'

'Flower! Why are you so bloody contrary sometimes?'

'It didn't.'

'What do you mean? Didn't you and Liam do your song?'

'No. They ran out of time and so we didn't do it. Anyway, Miss O'Neill has us down to do the Bella song.'

'Flower,' said Mick in a slow, disapproving way.

'We can't change it now,' I pleaded.

'Why not?'

I shrugged.

'The doctor said I can get out of here in time to come and see you.'

'I sure hope so.' I hadn't imagined Mick *not* being there.

'We each get one complimentary ticket. Mine is for you.'

'What about your parents?'

'They'll have to pay. *If* they come.'

'Well, I'm not coming unless you sing "Movin",' said Mick.

Forty-three

I pushed the key in the front door and quietly clicked it open. I could hear my parents talking in the kitchen, so I slipped down the corridor towards my room. I could tell by the tone, the tight cadence of their voices, that they were talking about something serious. Short sentences with hard consonants and taut vowels. I slowed down.

'It will be free in three weeks,' said my mother.

'Can't they wait until after the holiday?' asked my dad.

'No. Someone else is interested. If we don't take it—'

'It's so soon.'

'We haven't got much choice.'

'We still have a few possibilities here.'

'We can't be sure about it,' said my mother. 'And Ken needs help with a big house. The job's ours.'

'It's only for a month.'

'It's better than nothing.'

'Flower won't be happy.'

'She'll just have to go with the flow. She adapts pretty well.'

What? 'She adapts pretty well.' Is that what they think I do? They have no idea. Another move? Another school? I know I'm not Miss Popularity here, and Cat isn't really my close friend any more. But I can't leave Mick. And what about Liam? Liam? Does Liam really matter to me? Who would he have to play music with?

'Let's not mention anything to Flower just yet,' said my mother. 'It's not absolutely certain.'

'Where is she by the way?'

My cue for a quick and quiet disappearance into my room, with their words beating on my eardrums.

Well, I won't go! Not this time. They promised me! I'll stay with Mick. Or maybe Liam's mother will let me stay there. I'll plan it all and when my parents tell me that we're moving, I'll present them with a *fait accompli*. It's not as if I have a lot of stuff. I can easily fit it into a corner of Mick's flat. Or maybe I can share Liam's sister's room.

How can they do this to me again? My school uniform is still huge on me. She probably knew all along that we wouldn't be staying here! They never had any intention of staying. It was all a con!

They don't care about me. They never have. All they care about is one another. I'm just an inconvenience they have to think about every time they fail in their stupid business. They're both just losers.

There was a knock on the door. I shoved my earphones on my head. The door opened a crack. I pretended I didn't know anyone was there. I pretended I couldn't hear.

'Flower?'

It was my mother. I ignored her.

'Flower?'

She came and touched my shoulder. I pretended to be surprised.

'Supper's ready,' she said. She said it very gently. She always put on this gentle act when we were going to move. She thought it might somehow soften the blow. Well, it didn't work. It made it worse. She was really only trying to make herself feel better. Fat lot she cared about how I felt about it.

The three of us sat together at the table eating the usual. Pasta. Only this time my mother had bothered to buy a jar of pesto and some parmesan cheese to go with it. I normally love pesto but I didn't feel very hungry.

'What's the matter, Flower? You normally devour a jar of pesto in one sitting,' said my dad.

'Not hungry.'

'Your friend Mick wasn't on his stall today,' observed my mother.

'No.'

'What's happened?'

'He's in the hospital.'

'What's the matter?'

'Chest infection.'

Usually my parents talked to each other at the table. All this attention was overwhelming. Another sign that I was going to be uprooted again.

'I hope he's going to be all right,' said my mother. 'He's a lovely old codger.'

'He's going to be fine!' I cried, standing up and throwing my napkin down. 'And he's not an "old codger"!'

I ran to my room.

Forty-four

'Liam, can I come over and practise?'

Liam had finally deigned to answer his phone. However, the silence at the other end of the phone didn't bode well.

'Uh, well . . . problem . . . I've already done my hour of practice that my mum will put up with. She won't let me play again tonight.'

'Can you come out?'

'She won't let me come out either. How about to-morrow after school?'

'OK.' I said it as lamely as I could to make him feel really guilty.

'Are you OK, Weed?'

'Fine,' I said. 'See you tomorrow.'

I hung up. Maybe now he'll feel as bad as I do. But right now I needed to sing. And I couldn't do it in this house, with my mum and dad here. I opened my bedroom door. I could hear them clattering around in the kitchen still. They were washing up and putting stuff away. I didn't stop to listen to what they were saying. I tiptoed past and shut the front door behind me.

I ran. It was cold, but running warmed me up. I ran all the way out to the oak tree. Clouds were racing across the moon and I felt I was in league with them. Running the same race. And there was the oak tree. Bathed for a moment in moonlight and then lost in the sweeping darkness of a cloud.

I leaned against the tree, caught my breath and then I started to sing. I sang my song, my love song to this oak tree. It stayed here. It never moved. I loved it.

Shards of cloud across the sky
racing with my heart
chase away the dying day
another night creeps in

I lean my back against you
I know you're always there

Words pelt down like freezing rain
streaming down my face
wash away, drain away
Carry me away

Your branches sway above my head
Leaves sing a dying tune

Here and there I pace the day
looking for a map
scraps of paper flying by
catch upon a branch

I sit among your gnarled roots
I feel them hold the earth

Petals open full of hope

warming up my soul
smiles of a summer night
suddenly turn cold

I lean my back against you
I know you're always there

And then I sang 'Movin''. The words, the sound – they flowed right through me. I could feel them in my veins, my fingertips, behind my eyes. Filling me up and emptying me out. And then I felt better.

I sang all my songs – some two or three times. And there were now quite a few of them, so I don't know how long I was out there under that oak tree, with the clouds tearing across the sky. All silvery edges and black scraps. And my voice floating into the sky. I hadn't noticed the cold, until I started shivering. But I didn't mind. It was wonderful out there.

Forty-five

'I'll do "Movin'"' if Mick makes it on the night,' I said to Liam as we walked back to his house after school.

Liam just looked at me out of the corner of his eye.

'C'mon Liam! I *want* him to get better and come and see us. He will get better.'

'You sure?'

'I'm sure.'

And after last night, after singing out there in the field, by my oak tree – I wanted to sing my own song. At least I think I wanted to. Every time I thought about it too much, I started to get that stuttery feeling about it. If only I could just *do* it. When I didn't think about it, the singing just happened. I wouldn't think about it.

'Are you going to see him?' asked Liam.

'I'll go after our practice.'

And what a practice we had! Sometimes things just click. We did a couple of Bella songs to warm up and already I could feel that pulse, that beat of moments between us that was timed so perfectly. And sometimes, Liam did a little riff that he hadn't done before, and it felt just right. He dared. Then I dared. We pushed each other just a little bit further so that by the time we came to my songs we were hot. Not hot for each other. That's a disgusting thought. But just so ready to take my songs a little bit further. And maybe because I

155

was so raw from hearing my parents talking the night before – the words came from that part of me. They *were* me. They were the shape, the force, the sound of my hurt.

'Phew! You OK?' asked Liam.

'Yeah!'

I hadn't told him about hearing my parents talking about moving away.

'Let's leave that one for a while,' he said. 'It's so intense.'

But he was smiling. And for the first time I noticed how green his eyes were. This real emerald green, like you imagine the colour of ferns in a tropical forest. And that his rusty hair was all shiny, with glints of gold.

'The oak tree, then?' I said.

'OK!'

And we were off again. Split second touch. Vibrating at the same frequency. It was making me crazy with energy. I could have kept going all night, but Liam's mum called him for supper.

'Do I have to?' he called.

'All that creative energy needs some fuel,' she replied. 'Flower, do you want to stay for supper?'

'Thanks, but I'm going to see Mick at the hospital.'

We said goodbye, and I headed towards the hospital. I couldn't stop singing – until I passed someone who looked at me in the indulgent, slightly amused way they look at old people who are doing something eccentric that's put down to them being a bit doolally. So I stopped.

But I kept humming things in my head. It's weird how when you're singing, you don't even think about the words. You don't have to think about remembering them.

It's not like when you have to memorise a poem you don't like – when it's like you're speaking at the end of a conveyor belt and the words are being shunted along. You feel they are there, queuing up to come out. There's always the worry that the next one won't show up. But singing. The words flow out of you. You don't think. They just come. From somewhere. Where are they in that moment before your voice sings them? In your head? At the back of your throat? Floating around in the air waiting to be caught by your tongue? Inside. Just inside and then outside at the same time. Your mind and body so perfectly in tune, so to speak. I guess that's what it's like if you're a really good athlete (which I'm not). Somehow your mind and body work in harmony to perform the perfect move.

Singing is a feeling for me. And it makes me feel. Happy. Sad. Angry. Sexy. Sexy, even if the songs aren't about sex. It's strange, the way I sometimes get this feeling of strength that makes me feel sexy. Not like I want to go and snog Liam or anything. (Ashok maybe.) Not anything like that. But in a wider way. A walking down the street way. So how does that happen? I was thinking all of this when suddenly I realised I was already at the hospital. The same lady was on reception. She smiled and said hello. I ran up the stairs two at a time. Familiar faces greeted me. I was starting to feel at home here.

I turned down the corridor to Fleming Ward. I think Mick knew the sound of my footsteps because he seemed to call out my name before I even got in the door. But this time, no 'Flower!' hallooed across the low buzz of

157

hospital machines. In the corner, an empty bed. The song in my head skittered like the needle on one of Mick's records – when I had once been careless. Then silence in my head. Like the emptiness of the bed.

The old man beside Mick's bed was folded into white sheets of sleep. I looked around. I must have looked frantic, because a cracked voice from the other side of the room called out.

'It's OK, pet. He's just gone down to the shop.'

I wheeled around and at that moment, Mick strolled in, looking pleased as punch.

'Hello, Diva,' he said.

His voice was clear, not full of the cough. He looked so much better. His hair was combed and his robe was clean and pressed. How did he manage that?

'Mick!'

He took my arm and walked me over to the bed. I was taller than he was.

'Sit down,' he said, patting the edge of his bed. He sat down beside me.

'Stop gawping,' he said. 'I've got some news.'

I noticed that he hadn't said 'good' news. I sat down. Thoughts pulled tight in my head.

'I'm going home!' he beamed.

'When?' I cried. 'Now?'

'Tomorrow morning. One more night in here to make sure everything is still fine. Final checks first thing tomorrow. Then off I go.'

I threw my arms around his neck.

'Oh, Mick! That's great!'

'But he's not to stand out in the cold selling flowers for

at least at week!' said a voice behind me.

I turned. A young woman with a stethoscope around her neck smiled at us.

'You must be Flower,' she said.

She held out her hand.

'I'm Parveen. I've heard a lot about you. You're a singer?'

I felt my face getting hot.

'I like singing,' I muttered.

'So do I,' she said. 'But I'm not very good. Pity. I think sometimes a good song could do my patients more good than all the drugs I can give them.'

'Good idea!' chuckled Mick. 'The singing cure. I'm sure it would work for me.'

Parveen's pager started beeping. She shut it off.

'Well, you two take it easy. And I'll see you tomorrow morning, Mick. 'Bye, Flower.'

She breezed out.

'She's a Billie Holiday fan too,' said Mick, smiling after her.

'Maybe I could take the morning off school and come and get you tomorrow,' I said.

'Oh, no, you're not,' said Mick. 'You're not missing school on my account. They've got it all worked out. A community bus.'

'I'll come over right after school,' I said.

'That would be grand,' said Mick. 'But don't you look glowing and healthy tonight!'

'Liam and I had a really good practice.'

'So it's going well, is it?'

'Really well. And guess what?'

159

'What?'

'I've promised Liam that if you come to the performance, I'll do my own song.'

'It's just as well they've let me out then, isn't it?'

'If you're there, I can sing it for you. Then I won't get nervous, or frozen up by all the other people.'

Forty-six

'I saw your friend Mick back on his stall,' said my mother. She caught me as I slipped in the front door after a session with Liam.

'He asked me to give you these.'

She held out a small bunch of white freesias. Mick had been back home for five days. He still had a bad cough, but he said it was nothing. I knew he couldn't wait to get back to his beloved flowers. It was sooner than he should have, but I wasn't surprised. I had spent most evenings with him – after Liam and I practised. We played music, talked and sometimes I sang. It was just like before he went into the hospital. Tonight I had an English essay to finish and so I couldn't go. I took the freesias and put them in a tall skinny vase. I was about to carry them off to my room when my mother spoke.

'Flower.'

She spoke in that gentle, I've-got-bad-news voice. I didn't want to hear what she was going to say. I carried on towards my room.

My mother followed me into my room.

'Flower. We've got to talk.'

'I've got an essay to write. It's got to be in tomorrow.'

'Your father and I have had to make a difficult decision.'

'Can't it wait?'

'It's important.'

'OK. Surprise me then. You're going to buy this flat? We're going to have something besides pasta for supper? You're going to take me on a holiday? That *would* be a surprise,' I snorted.

'Flower. Don't be so mean.'

But I wanted to be mean to her. They were going to wrench me away from Mick. They were going to deprive Liam of his singing partner. They were doing it all over again.

'Do you think I'm so stupid that I don't know what you're going to tell me?'

'We haven't had an easy time here.'

'Oh really? Like *I* have? But luckily I "adapt easily". I can just go with the flow. Never mind that I've made a really good friend. Even if he is an "old codger". Never mind that I'm supposed to be singing in Miss O'Neill's music night. Never mind that Liam won't have anyone to perform with.'

'You didn't tell me about any music night.'

'Yes, I did. But you don't remember.'

'You're singing?'

'Is that such a big surprise?'

'When is it?'

'What do you care? You'll be living in Wales by then!'

'What do you know about that?'

'You don't even notice when I'm here to overhear you!'

'What do you know?'

'You tell me!'

'We're not going for three weeks.'

'Well, I'm not going!'

'Flower, be reasonable.'

'Why am I always the one who has to be reasonable?'

'We can talk about this another time. When you've calmed down.'

'It was you who wanted to talk about it now. I wanted to write my English essay.'

'We'll talk about it tomorrow.' My mother turned towards the door. When she was just outside, I lunged towards it and slammed it hard behind her.

I hated her! I hated my father! They did whatever they wanted. They only cared about one another. What about me?

In the next half hour I scribbled down a verse that they would hate.

Forty-seven

The music night was now only two nights away. By concentrating on my English essay I thought I could put it out of my mind. But after my argument with my mother I couldn't concentrate at all. My brain felt like it was being beaten up. Thoughts, like big fists, were hitting me from every direction. Mick's illness. Moving to Wales. The music night. And feeling really really angry with my parents.

So I went out and went to my website. I had neglected it recently and I felt a bit guilty. Like I had abandoned my cubs.

There were lots of emails from little kids asking stupid questions, but I felt I had to answer them. I held off the moment when I would click into the Amur Project website. I was afraid that something bad had happened to Tashi. And Borya. I built up my courage and clicked the mouse. Nothing. No news. Their radio collars were still beeping so they were still out there somewhere, but neither Tashi nor Borya had been seen for ages.

The next two days were impossible. I tried to block out my anger about moving. I promised myself I wouldn't get miserable until after the music night. I had a great evening with Mick on the Thursday. I sang him my new song – the one I scribbled the night I'd had my argument with my mother. He said he remembered feeling like that when his parents apprenticed him to a plumber. He'd hated it. Luckily it had only lasted a few months. Finally they let him take on the flower stall.

'I wish *my* parents were a little more understanding,' I said.

'What's up?' he asked.

I didn't want to tell him about moving but I had to tell someone.

'My parents are moving in three weeks.'

There was a long silence.

'No wonder your song is so strong,' he said.

And we had left it at that.

And I was sure Mick would think of something. He would work out a way for me to stay. I gave him a big hug and promised to come by the next evening at half past six. We would have tea. He would calm me down and then we'd walk together to the school. I'd be ready for the big night.

I headed home for a sleepless night – a bit like the night before Christmas, only mixed up with the excitement were these sticky clods of fear which lumped through my gut like fat ugly turds.

I didn't really wake up in the morning. I just sort of shifted from a horizontal state of total anxiety to a vertical one. I was a strange mixture of a zombie on the outside and a cauldron on the inside. I couldn't eat breakfast. I couldn't even wait for school to talk to Liam. I phoned him so early I woke him up.

'Weed?' said Liam's drowsy voice.

'Liam! Have you actually been sleeping?' I squealed into the phone.

'Yes. And I would be now,' he said, 'if you hadn't woken me up.'

'But tonight's the night!'

I could hear him sighing at the other end of the line.

'Go and have some breakfast,' he said.

'I can't eat.'

'You need to keep your strength up.'

At that moment, a huge wave of something like nausea swept over me. A cold chill. It soaked through me. Fear. Dread. Panic. It was so real. So outside my control.

'I don't think I can do it, Liam,' I shivered.

'Meet me at the café at the corner of Drummond and Thorpedale in fifteen minutes,' said Liam.

And so we sat down fifteen minutes later at an old cracked yellow-topped table. Steamy windows blocked out the grey morning. Liam bought some toast and I managed to eat a piece. I couldn't understand how he could be so calm.

The rest of the day was a nightmare. Teachers kept asking me questions which I didn't even hear until they started shouting at me for: (a) living on another planet, (b) not getting enough sleep (which was true), (c) leaving my brain at home. Only Miss O'Neill, in the last class of the day, let me off the hook. She asked me to sort through the text books for the next term; a mindless task which soothed my nerves but then reminded me that I probably wouldn't be here next term. Except I kept hoping that Mick would think of something to make it all right.

Finally the bell sounded. I dropped the pile of books I had just spent half an hour sorting through.

'Just leave them, Flower,' said Miss O'Neill. 'I'm sure you have more important things to do right now.'

She smiled.

'And I'll be cheering you on tonight!'

'Thanks,' I mumbled.

Liam grabbed me by the hand.

'C'mon. We've got an hour of good practice time before my mother gets home.'

'Don't play yourselves out,' called Miss O'Neill as Liam pulled me out the door.

But we didn't play ourselves out. We warmed up well enough but when it came to doing my songs, everything went wrong. It wasn't Liam. It was me. I got the timing wrong. I started in the wrong key. My phrasing was haywire.

'It's not going to work,' I wailed.

'Never mind,' said Liam. 'We'll save it for tonight.'

'There won't be any tonight,' I said.

'We'll be great,' argued Liam.

'I won't be able to get up there,' I moaned.

'Oh shut up!' said Liam.

'What?!'

'Stop being a drama queen!'

Forty-eight

Liam just didn't understand what it was like to have stage fright. It was OK for him. He *liked* getting up there in front of people. I was seriously considering going out to the oak tree and staying there for the rest of the night. The only thing that stopped me was the thought of disappointing Mick.

I went home first. I had decided to wear the top that Cat had given me for my birthday. It was the only one I had that was at all sparkly. I was making a mess of ironing it (it was really hard to iron around and in between the sequin pattern), when the front door opened and my parents came in.

'You going out?' asked my mother.

I couldn't believe it.

'I was going to order in some pizza for tonight. Special treat,' she bleated.

'Sorry,' I said in the most sarcastic voice I could. (It came easily to me, actually.) 'But I'm performing at the school tonight.'

I didn't look at her.

'Oh my God!' said my mother in a quick rush of breath.

'What's the matter?' asked my father.

'Flower's music night at school.'

'We won't have the pizzas,' said my father. 'We'll go to the school.'

'It's all sold out,' I sneered, turned on my heel and headed towards my room.

I could hear their anxious mutterings in the kitchen. Good! Let them feel guilty. I pulled on my jeans, slid on my top and started to brush my hair. There was a knock on the door.

'Flower,' said my mother.

I did *not* want to talk to my parents.

I crammed my brush and my music into my bag and headed for the door. My parents were just pushing it open in that tentative way they do when they're feeling like naughty children.

'I'm late,' I said. 'I've got to get going.'

I brushed past them.

'Flower! Wait! I'm sorry—'

I grabbed my jacket and shut the door behind me.

It was freezing outside. As I buttoned up my jacket, I thought how it nice and warm it would be at Mick's. How glad he would be to see me. How unlike my parents he was.

We would have a bit of time together before we had to set off for the school. Time to listen to a bit of Billie. If I could just sit there with Mick and listen to her sing 'Georgia on My Mind', it would calm me down. It was like having a massage, listening to that song.

I turned the corner by Mick's flower stall. The string of lights was blazing away and it was still open. Didn't he know what time it was? I couldn't see him. He must be on the other side by his old wooden chair.

'Flower!! Flower!'

Mrs Bhat rushed towards me.

'Mick!! It is terrible. He has just been rushed to the hospital by ambulance.'

Her face was all pushed and pulled into a mess of panicked eyes and lips.

'He collapsed. Fell down. He was so grey. I phoned the ambulance.'

'When? When did it happen?'

'I don't know. An hour ago maybe? I've been trying to find your phone number. Mick said you were coming.'

'But he was fine last night!' I cried.

'And today as well. He was so happy to be going to see you at the school tonight.'

I started to run towards the hospital.

Forty-nine

I ran into the hospital reception. People. Signs. Sharply-focused one minute. A blur the next. I rushed across the hard shiny floor. I headed for Fleming Ward. Idiot! Mick wouldn't be there. But where? A & E. That's where Mick would be. But where was that?

I heard a familiar voice.

'What's the matter, dear?'

I whirled around. It was the friendly receptionist I knew from previous visits to see Mick.

It was then that I burst into tears.

She came out from behind her desk and put her arm around my shoulder. I remember her guiding me somewhere. It must have been back behind her big counter.

'Tell me what's the matter. Maybe I can do something.' I heard her voice through a storm of tears, helplessness, panic.

'Mick . . . my friend Mick . . . the ambulance . . . he's here somewhere. He collapsed. Is he going to be all right?'

'We'll find out,' she said. 'Have this glass of water.'

I was vaguely aware of the receptionist making calls, of hearing fragments. Mick Flanagan. Young friend. She's very upset. ICU? Yes. I'll get Charlie to bring her up.

The receptionist touched my shoulder.

'I'm going to get one of the porters to take you up to see Mick. He's been asking for you. He's in intensive care.'

'Is that bad?'

'It means he's being really well taken care of.'

An elderly man appeared. He reminded me a bit of Mick.

'My name's Charlie. Come with me, pet,' he said.

More corridors, people in bathrobes, a mother carrying a child with cowboy pyjamas, swing doors. Lots of swing doors.

'Flower.'

I turned. It was Parveen. The doctor I'd met the last night I visited Mick in hospital.

'Thanks, Charlie,' she said. 'I'll go the rest of the way with Flower.'

'He's OK, isn't he?' I burbled.

Parveen didn't look at me for a moment.

She took my arm.

'He's had a very bad heart attack.'

'But he's OK?! The receptionist said he's in intensive care. They take good care of you there.'

'He was still very weak from his chest infection.'

'What does that mean?'

'He's dying, Flower.'

I nearly fell down. The lines of the corridor seemed to zoom away from us.

'Not Mick. No, he can't! He can't die!'

Parveen held onto me. She stopped and looked into my eyes.

'He knows he's dying. He wants to see you.'

Something in the way she held me in her look, steadied me. I gulped. Took some deep breaths.

'Can you do it?'

I nodded.

'Come with me, then.'

172

Through a swing door. A room. Lots of machines. Screens. Lights. And on a huge bed. Mick. Smaller than I'd ever seen him before. He turned towards me. His eyes were closed.

'Flower!' he whispered. He smiled.

I walked over to the side of the bed. His hand felt for mine. We held hands. His breathing was all shallow and spluttery.

'I'm not going to make it to your music night,' he said.

I squeezed his hand. I couldn't trust myself to speak.

'But you go out there and sing. Promise me you'll do that?'

'Without you there, Mick, I don't—'

He put up his hand to stop me talking.

'I promise,' I said.

'I'll be with you in spirit.'

He smiled.

'I want you to have my music collection. And I want your mum and dad to have my flower stall.'

This time he squeezed my hand.

'That way you won't have to move to Wales.'

His hand slackened.

'Will you sing to me? The oak tree song?'

And so I sang. Quietly. Holding Mick's hand. Watching his eyelids flutter. Wishing my voice could make his heart strong. Strong as an oak tree.

As I reached the last notes, Mick smiled.

'You've got soul,' he whispered.

And he stopped breathing.

Fifty

I don't know how long I sat there. Holding Mick's hand. It was so strange. I didn't want to leave him.

Finally Parveen touched my shoulder.

She undid my hand from Mick's. The moment she did that, it all flooded out. Tears, snot, howls, hiccups. Heat surged up behind my eyes.

Parveen put her arms around me and let me cry into her shoulder.

'He was lucky to have a friend like you with him,' she said.

'He wasn't lucky!' I howled. 'He died!'

She didn't say anything. She just held me until I stopped. Then, once again, she looked at me and said very quietly, 'Well, I hope someone is there to sing me a song like that when I go.'

I wiped my eyes. Parveen handed me a tissue.

'Why don't you call your parents?' she said. 'Do you have a phone?'

I shook my head.

'There's a public phone in the waiting room downstairs. Do you have any change?'

I nodded.

'I'll go down and phone.'

Parveen walked me to the staircase.

'Thanks,' I said.

'He was proud of you,' she said. 'Don't you forget that.'

174

I had no idea where I was going. I had no idea how much time had passed. All I knew was, that during that time, Mick's life had ended. I still couldn't believe it. I didn't know what it meant – for someone to be alive and warm one minute, and dead the next. Where were they? Where had they gone in that moment?

Suddenly I was in a busy waiting room. Full of people. Sitting. Waiting. Children crying. Playing games. Parents holding babies. I saw a phone. A man with very shiny, slick-backed hair was using it. I dug into my purse for some coins and took up a position close enough to the phone to stake my claim as the next in line.

I got lost in the strange collision of life carrying on and the profound finality of Mick's death. I kept seeing a wave sliding down a shelf of sand and the water sinking away into the sand. Bits of plastic and junk rolling down the sand.

When my thoughts came back to the waiting room, the man was still on the phone. Now I desperately wanted to talk to Liam. I needed him to know Mick had died. I waited some more. I was getting annoyed at this man. He knew I was waiting. He glanced across at me. I folded my arms across my chest and frowned. Finally he hung up.

The receiver was warm against my ear. His body heat. Yuck.

I dialled Liam's mobile. It rang. And rang some more. Where are you, Liam?

Finally Liam's voice.

'H'lo?'

'Liam. It's me.'

'Weed! Where the hell are you? We've missed our spot on the schedule. It's part way into the second half. Miss O'Neill said if you turned up she would let us play last spot of the night. What the hell is happening? Are you all right?'

The rush of Liam's anger, frustration and finally his concern splashed over me like cold water.

'I'll tell you all about it when I get there. How much time have I got?'

'Twenty-five minutes! Tops!'

'I'll be there.'

I burst into a blast of cold night air and ran. In the sky the moon raced between the trails of silver cloud, just like it had that wonderful night at the oak. Tears streamed from my eyes.

Fifty-one

'Weed!'

Liam was waiting by the stage door.

'Ashok and Lenny are on. They're the last act before us. What happened?'

'Can we do the oak tree song instead of "Movin'"?'

'But we worked on 'Movin''. That's our song.'

'I know, but this is really important.'

'What?'

I took a big breath.

'Mick died tonight. I just sang it to him before he died. I need to sing it again.'

'Oh, Weed. I'm so sorry.'

Liam put his arms around me. He held me for a long time. It felt so good. But I had to break away before I started crying again.

'I'll tell you all about it later.'

I touched his cheek.

'We'll do this one for him.'

Huge applause exploded from the audience. I could see Ashok, Lenny and BJ taking their bows and punching the air. So full of life, energy. Ashok still so gorgeous. I suddenly felt a huge current pulse along every nerve in my body.

Miss O'Neill went out onto the stage to introduce us.

'Are you OK?' said Liam.

'Scared shitless,' I said.

He grinned and nudged me onto the stage.

I don't know how I got to the middle of the stage. I just remember touching the mike and saying,

'This song is called "Your Heart is an Oak" – and this is for Mick.'

I looked at Liam, he nodded and hit the first chord. My brain dropped into my heart, or my heart flew up into my brain – that's the only way I can explain it. Because everything that I was feeling poured into the words. There was no difference between me and the sounds and the energy that Liam and I were making. We were so much in sync. And while I had sung a gentle version of the song to Mick, this was something else. This is what Mick would have liked to hear in this big wide world, where his spirit lives on. This version *was* his spirit living on.

I wanted to go on singing forever. To keep Mick's spirit soaring above me. To feel Liam's guitar stirring my heart. For the three of us to ride through the night on this wave of music. Music that was us.

Too soon I could feel my voice, Liam's guitar rising to meet in the final crescendo, and then fall away like that last leaf of autumn.

Then it was silent. And the silence held. For an awfully long time. I looked into the black, blurry mass that was the audience. For a moment I thought that maybe they'd all left.

Then someone clapped. Then someone else. And suddenly the entire place erupted. This huge sound beat against our ears. Our chests. Our whole bodies.

I looked at Liam. His face was filled with a big sweaty smile.

We bowed and walked off the stage.

The clapping got louder.

Miss O'Neill pushed us back onto the stage.

'Go on. Another bow!'

Back onto the stage. The clapping thundered. Someone shouted, 'More!' Then someone else shouted, 'Encore!'

We bowed. We started back towards the wings.

'More!'

Miss O'Neill signalled for us to go back.

'Play another one!' she shouted.

I looked at Liam.

'"Movin'"', he mouthed above the noise.

I went back to the microphone. Liam played a chord. The audience went quiet. Liam looked at me. He hit that first hard, sharp chord and we were off. And now this song meant something different from before. Before tonight. Before Mick dying. Before this performance. Now it was a mixture – of going somewhere, tinged with sadness of leaving something and someone behind. And grief. And I guess that's what I felt. Feelings are so complicated.

another place
another face
never time to find my place
moving on
moving on
leaving friends behind
words fly by
too fast to catch
why won't you ever listen?

moving on
moving on
snatch my thoughts away

dreaming eyes
streaming by
too fast for me to see
moving on
moving on
leaving me behind

with those goodbyes
I lose a world
will I find another?
moving on
moving on
everything's adrift

Liam's playing was brilliant. Hard and driving and then soft, like the flutter of birds' wings. I could feel my words floating on his chords and then being driven onwards. Or at least that's what it felt like. To be able to connect with the world this way was wonderful.

Just as we finished the last verse I looked at Liam and stepped up to the mike.

'And this is for my parents,' I said.

Liam's guitar screamed and I began to sing.

Leave me out
Just leave me out
Three can play at this game

Go away
Just drive away
The road's too dark to see

And then, before we knew it, we were there on the last bars. Holding onto them. Unwilling to let go of the song. But just at the right moment, we did.

More huge applause. I couldn't believe it. They liked it. My parents weren't there but I'd needed to say that.

Fifty-two

When we got backstage, the other performers formed a half circle around us and applauded. Miss O'Neill gushed.

'That was amazing. Flower, you are one helluva singer. And Liam, you are one helluva of a guitar player.'

Suddenly Ashok and Lenny were there at the front of the crowd. They were clapping too. Ashok. All those times I had begged him in my thoughts to look at me. To see me. Smile at me. Now here he was. His dark chocolate eyes holding me in all their deliciousness. I felt a current cross the air between us.

'You were great!' he mouthed over the clapping.

'Thanks!' I mouthed back.

Suddenly I felt I had this power. It had spilled over from the stage. It felt so good.

As the clapping died down, people said really complimentary things: 'You guys were great. I really liked those songs. How do you think up words like that?' Cat slipped through the crowd and wrapped herself around Lenny.

Ashok was quiet and when there was a pause, he said,

'Wow. That's what I call Flower Power.'

That was s-o-o-o-o corny. But coming from Ashok, it almost sounded cool. I think I blushed. Then came the bombshell.

'Would you join our band?' he asked.

'What?' screamed a voice in my head. 'Is he really asking me to join the most popular, the most creative, the

182

best local band around? This beautiful guy whom I've lusted after ever since I clapped eyes on him?'

I saw Cat look at Ashok like she might kill him. What sweet revenge it would be to be up there on stage with him while Cat was stuck down in the audience. Then she turned to me and beamed.

'You were great, Flower!'

For a moment I felt ashamed.

'Thanks,' was all I could manage.

Then my imagination fast forwarded to No. 1 hits on Radio 1, concerts at big London venues – all with Ashok.

Then out of the corner of my eye I caught sight of Liam. He was trying to look somewhere that wasn't caught up in the exchange of looks that was zapping around this little crowd. His red guitar was still around his neck. I thought of Mick. Friendship. Loyalty.

I flashed my best smile at Ashok.

'Thanks. That's a great offer, but Liam and I are going to stick together. Aren't we, Liam?'

Epilogue

When I think back to that night, and all that's happened since, it's so confusing and complicated. I was feeling so many things – all mixed up together. So out of my head with sadness, so much at a loss about Mick, and at the same time, so full of power, the pleasure of all that applause, the happiness of Ashok's admiration. The funny thing was, my parents *were* at the concert that night. They talked their way into a sold-out house. So they heard my songs. They heard the verse that I dedicated to them. They even showed up backstage after the big fuss had died down. When I introduced them to Miss O'Neill she said, 'You must be so proud of Flower.' They put their arms around each other and grinned lovingly into one another's eyes. 'Yes! That's our daughter,' they said. Typical. I don't even think they got it – my verse for them. But, as I said before, I'm not one to dwell on the misfortune of my parents.

They are in the process of taking over Mick's flower stall. It's not straightforward, despite the fact that Mick left a will of sorts giving it to them. I don't understand all the ins and outs, but Mick's family isn't too happy about the stall going to my parents. They are contesting the will or something like that. The stupid thing is, his family don't even want to come down and look after it. They want to sell it. In the meantime, my mum and dad are looking after it. So we haven't had to move – not yet anyway. They're really happy and the flower business is thriving. They still act as if I don't exist most of the time, but it doesn't matter because now I've got my music and lots of friends. Liam and I did a gig at a small youth centre. It was great. I will die if the stall doesn't work out and we have to move. I can't bear the thought of moving on again.

And there's good news on the tiger front. Tashi and Borya are alive and well and padding through the snowy forests of eastern Russia. One day, they'll have their own cubs. Maybe *panthera tigris altaica* will survive after all.

I miss Mick so much. I still take a bunch of freesias from the stall every Tuesday and put them in a vase. I inhale their sweet scent and think of Mick.

He left me his CD and record collection, and every time I play Billie, or Nina and the others, Mick is there, smiling until the gap shows between his teeth.

But most of all, he lives on in the music that Liam and I make together. If it hadn't been for Mick, I don't think I would have ever got up on that stage and discovered the power that Liam and I have to connect to the world through our music.

'You've got soul,' Mick said. And now, I'm discovering what he meant.